# CANDLE WAX AND SUNLIGHT

## A DEATHLESS LOVE NOVELLA

**ZORA FOX**

# WELCOME TO THE EIGHT REALMS

A land of gods and goddesses—a savage, beautiful collection of islands in the Corae Sea. The stories here are violent, with explicit sexual content not intended for anyone under 18. These books about deathless love feature dark, often twisted romances. Enter at your own risk.

ZENIA

Ruled by Thenios, God-King of lightning

## APHRISO

Ruled by Cytherea, goddess of pleasure

## ERISET

Contested land, ruled by Ares and Bellona, god and goddess of war

## MENOS

Ruled by Scira, goddess of wisdom

## NALIA

Ruled by Basileus, god of the ocean

## HYPERION

Ruled by Lox, god of the sun

## KANTHAROS

Ruled by Vesta, goddess of hearth and home

## FAR REALM

Ruled by Hades, god of the dead

Content warnings for this story of deathless love: explicit sex, wax play, orgies, abusive relationships, sexual assault, injury, brief instances of strong violence, strong language

# I

# JACIN

Roshan knelt in front of me, painting my calf gold. The paintbrush tickled. Or maybe I was simply on edge because the King finally wanted to see me.

I held my hand out, rotating it slowly in the lamplight. It shone brighter than everything around it, the gold shining in contrast to the dark red room where I spent most of my time. I looked like metal compared to the soft hangings and pillows and baskets of "accentuations" that littered the room. That was the name Roshan used, anyway, and the small number of other palace attendants. Really, they were little bottles filled with oils and tins of scent and drinks labeled with things I blushed to look at. Not to mention the objects that set my imagination aflame.

The gold paint had to be part of King Lox's plan. I'd never seen any of his other consorts, but the Sun King enjoyed light. Like the sun, he glowed. His magnificence chased away darkness in the kingdom. I had to be a fitting partner for him.

My stomach tightened painfully.

"Please don't move," said Roshan.

"I'm sorry. I'll try not to."

I stood as still as I could. Only the tip of the paintbrush grazed my feet, never Roshan's hand, and the bristles tickled.

It wasn't just my nerves.

I bit my lip hard, realizing a second afterward that my lips had been painted too. Hopefully I hadn't spoiled Roshan's work. My assistant didn't visit often, except to deliver food and such, and he wasn't talkative. Sometimes he acted like he didn't enjoy his job at all, though he never said that. Since he was the only person I saw regularly, I wanted to crack through his tough exterior so we could become friends.

When he reached a particularly ticklish spot, my foot jerked.

Roshan cursed and reared back. "My excellent ray, the Sun God's favorite," he recited through his teeth, "I almost touched you."

"I'm sorry," I repeated. "My feet are ticklish." I grimaced at him in apology.

He pushed a mass of dark, curly hair out of his face before carefully leaning forward again to finish the job. He had beautiful hair and beautiful skin. I'd learned he had a daughter, but he didn't like to talk to me, so I hadn't learned much else. I didn't even know if he was a demi-god. Or a full god. That thought hadn't even occurred to me. It was all far above a mere human like me, even if I was chosen several years ago for King Lox. Maybe Roshan was a demi-god and that was the reason he didn't want to become my friend. To him, I only lasted a second.

I had to get my mind off my upcoming presentation and

ticklish foot, though, so I tried again. "Roshan, is this what you do with all the King's consorts?"

He didn't look up. "I only serve you."

"But you can see more of the palace," I insisted. "Have you seen any other gold people?"

"The gold is just for meetings with the King," he murmured, clenching his free hand into a fist at his side to keep from touching me.

My next question burned my tongue. "For this meeting..."

He slipped the paintbrush between my toes. The most challenging part came next, when I'd have to stand on one leg to present the sole of my foot. That would be even more difficult than when he'd painted my groin half an hour ago. My cock had started to respond to the touch of the brush, but I'd stood still as a statue otherwise. Embarrassment was the only obstacle to get that done. Roshan regularly saw me naked. The embarrassing part was standing this close to someone, having them touch me. Sort of. With the brush, at least.

I hadn't been touched by living hands in six years.

I shut my eyes tight. "In this meeting, what exactly does the King expect me to do? I want to be ready."

Roshan tapped my anklebone with the brush, and I lifted my foot, wishing for something to hold onto. "He doesn't confide in me," he scoffed.

"But you know, don't you?" I pressed.

Finally, Roshan leaned back on his heels and looked up at me. "The Sun God does what pleases him, but I believe this meeting is like all the other firsts."

My heart thumped hard and fast behind my ribs. "What's... usual?"

"He wants you to learn. Watch and learn."

My blood didn't cool at the thought of *watching*, but anxiety didn't sprint so fast around my head. "Thank you." I scanned the room, my eyes skipping to each filled basket. When I first arrived at eighteen, I was told those baskets were for the King should he wish to visit. I'd waited breathlessly for months. Then years. And now, at last, he summoned me. "Are you... with someone? Here at the palace?" I asked Roshan.

"Not at the palace."

I waited for more, but he didn't go on. Instead, he blew the paint dry on the sole of one foot, which felt like torture. His face was too close. My foot wanted to kick out so bad it almost felt involuntary, but I breathed through it, shuddering a little when he instructed me to put my foot down.

In a couple more silent minutes, Roshan finished painting. I was golden for the Sun King. He didn't have to touch up my lip, thank the gods.

After putting away his tools, he led me to the back of my chamber, pushed aside the heavy curtain, and unlocked the door. We were about the same height, which could mean he was a tall human like me, or else a short deathless one. His fingers moved gracefully as he turned the key. They'd never given me a key. In an emergency, they would come fetch me, they said.

My breath shallowed as I followed Roshan. The hallway we entered was blinding bright—white and gold. No heavy curtains or scents. Music filtered through the air. It was beautiful, like the mornings I remembered as a child, when the sun would rise and turn the sky pale blue and orange. The instruments even replicated the feeling the cool dawn air sweeping across skin. It wasn't that I wanted to return home, exactly, but I wanted to see a sunrise again if I could. Maybe I could ask Roshan if that was possible for a consort of the King.

Even as the thought crossed my mind, I knew what he'd say. No. I was too precious to risk. I was reserved for one sun alone.

My throat bobbed. Today, I'd meet my king. This was the moment I'd waited for so long.

The hallway opened into a vast circular room many times the size of my chamber. Stylized golden suns hung suspended from huge chains on the ceiling. Multiple stories, maybe seven, rose and up and up. A few of the stories were rimmed in glass, so I could see people moving inside—an enormous array of people, mostly bronze-skinned and dark-haired, which was typical of Hyperion, but there were also half-reptile demi-gods and slender beings taller than any I'd seen in real life.

This palace was the beating heart of Hyperion. The lovely song ended and music changed. It came from a group of female musicians on the opposite side of the room, all pale and curvy, like sisters.

I wanted to watch them, but Roshan led us away.

Men and women stared as we passed. All wore clothes except for me. All of them kept their distance so they didn't accidentally touch me.

I gave an awkward half-smile to a few people, but no one offered a genuine smile back. When I caught Roshan glaring at me, I stopped looking around, focusing only on following him carefully and obediently.

He rounded a corner, then another—how big was this place?—and at last reached an ornate ivory column inlaid with gold and silver. When the light hit them just right, the carvings in the column showed a variety of scenes.

King Lox, larger than the people around him, ordering music to be played.

King Lox rising into the air like the sun itself.

King Lox, glowing, surrounded by worshippers on their faces.

King Lox, mouth open in ecstasy as three people knelt around him, the strongest-looking one clearly sucking on his—

"This is the most excellent ray, the Sun God's favorite, Jacin, who has been summoned," Roshan said.

I realized a woman stood guard beside the pillar. She looked as war-like as people from Eriset, the kingdom to the north caught in a centuries-long conflict between the ruling gods. Her gray eyes narrowed at Roshan but turned softer with surprise when she looked at me.

"I expected you," she said in a rock-hard voice. Her gaze dipped down my body.

I'd been told not to wear clothes, right? Hopefully, I hadn't done anything wrong. Even though this woman said what I wanted to hear—that King Lox waited for me—her tone said the opposite. If I was the Sun God's favorite, why did this guard look at me with... whatever this was? Suspicion, maybe?

She held out an armored hand. In it was a gnarled wooden staff too short to be useful to her.

I frowned at it. I'd expected her to have a dagger, or, I didn't know.

"Lay your hand on the staff," Roshan instructed.

I obeyed, laying my hand on the knobby end away from the guard's fingers.

The room with the massive pillar sucked into itself like a whirlpool. Right before everything squeezed into breathless, panicky blackness, I heard the guard say, "Don't let go."

I gripped with my fingers, but didn't move my hand any higher on the staff. The darkness crushed, but I could still feel the object beneath my fingertips.

*Don't let go. Don't let go.*

If I did, I would die. I knew it.

I couldn't breathe. My legs kicked air. I thrashed like a swimmer before—

We landed.

My feet hit solid ground and I gasped for breath, fingers trembling on the end of the staff. I was somewhere else.

"Release the staff," Roshan whispered, as if I'd done something impolite and needed correcting.

Had he just experienced that sensation too? Was this normal? I felt like I was walking around outside my body. So many months of nothing and now this. I almost laughed.

I forced myself to let go and take in the new space. The pillar I'd seen before rose to my right, tapered a little smaller. Maybe this was up on the top floor. The round room, not quite as large as mine, had a cluster of bright lights dropping from the center, illuminating a raised platform. Sky-blue cushions and pillows made the round platform like a bed or lounge. Along the opposite wall from where I stood was an enormous water feature. A quarter of the room ran with water that slipped over carvings on the wall, all depicting King Lox and his works, like the pillar did. Everything smelled sharp and musky. It made my mouth water. The floors were dark wood and, at the center of the dais, a figure glowed.

My mouth dropped open.

The Sun King.

He was tall, like all the deathless, and incredibly handsome. He wore a thin piece of white fabric pinned at the shoulder with a sunburst. Golden hair curled around his ears, just a shade lighter than mine. A rock jumped into my throat. I had something in common with the god. And I was his favorite. He'd finally called for me.

Beside me, Roshan fell on his face.

My skin zinged uncomfortably. Was I supposed to do the same thing? The guard didn't bow like that. And wasn't it better to stand to be presented to him? Sweat formed at my temple.

"My king," said the guard, tucking the gnarled staff into a specially made pouch at her side, "this is Jacin." Her tone was flat, but she gestured, open-palmed, at me.

"Jacin." The King caressed the syllables. He walked down the shallow steps toward me. I held my breath, inclining my head.

His pale golden eyes raked over me and he reached out.

When I flinched back, the King chuckled. It was a soothing noise. "No need to fear." His fingertips grazed my jaw.

The contact—my first in so long—buzzed along my blood. My whole body woke up, longing for more.

"Such a pretty one," the King crooned, swiping a thumb along my bottom lip as he observed me. "And eager." His gaze dropped to where I'd half-hardened at his touch.

I didn't even have the sense to be embarrassed. Mostly, I felt too overwhelmed.

The King's hand dropped. I missed its warmth on my face. "Very good," he said, clipped.

King Lox returned to the raised platform, lifted his eyes to the lights, inhaled deeply, and said, "Let them in."

The guard moved purposefully around the room, opening a set of two doors. Roshan still hadn't risen from where he bowed at my side.

Through the doors poured six naked, gold-painted young men, all beautiful in different ways. They strode to join the Sun King at the platform, as confident as dancers who had learned a routine.

Whatever was special about me faded. I had no right to feel disappointed. I was still his favorite, right? I just had to learn.

Focusing hard on the lighted platform, I tried to remember every movement, every touch. A muscular male unclipped the fabric from the King's shoulder, reverently folded it, and set it to the side. The god was the most beautiful among them, shining with his own light. He looked like a statue, ancient and young at the same time, his body carved from marble. Hands stroked and embraced him from every side. He pulled one in for a deep kiss while others knelt in front of him.

My stomach flipped. I couldn't believe I was watching this, that it was allowed. My cheeks and neck blazed, but I couldn't, *wouldn't*, look away.

King Lox all but disappeared among the mass of writhing, muscular bodies. One of them grasped a large bottle of oil and thumbed off the top. He soaked his hands with it and passed it along. Each consort rubbed the oil over themselves, each other, the King... They shone like purest gold.

The King moaned, face tipping up. My blood raced as I traced which person had given him that reaction. It was the male on his knees, now pressing the King's cock down his throat.

I bit my lip hard, trying to be a good learner, but growing stiff and painful and feeling every second how ignorant I was.

How was that one pleasing the King so well? When the bodies parted enough for me to see, I squinted at the one on his knees. His lips suctioned around the King's length as he bobbed.

*Okay, okay...*

Maybe I'd burst into flames.

The King pushed one down on his hands and knees facing me, shoving the man off his cock to make room. Still caressed by hands everywhere, King Lox, dripping with oil, thrust his hard dick into the man's ass. He rocked back and forth. I couldn't keep up with all the movements. The King gritted his teeth, plunging deep, and the man groaned loudly with pleasure. For some reason, the others started sighing and moaning too—even the ones who weren't being touched at all. Maybe their pleasure was connected to the King's.

The sights and sounds and smells all made my cock ache. I wanted to pump myself to ease the tension, but the King had brought me here to learn. Besides, no one else was allowed to touch me, so it was probably a bad idea to touch myself in front of the King.

His eyes met mine.

I couldn't help it. I gave a quiet gasp.

His gaze welcomed me. Did this mean...? Did he want me up there with him?

I stepped forward, awkward from being so turned on. My calf brushed something soft.

*Shit*! I hadn't looked down before I moved. My leg had touched Roshan.

His face whipped up angrily, eyes blown wide with fear.

Before I could open my mouth to apologize, explain that it was an accident, the guard swung a weapon hard at his head.

"No!"

But my word was cut off. Blinding pain cut through my leg. She moved so fast, I couldn't see what weapon it was, only felt the slice, the crunch reverberating through my body.

I fell next to Roshan, whose face was a mass of crushed flesh and blood. Bile rose in my throat. Before the piercing pain crested, I slitted open my eyes to see King Lox give an orgasmic yell.

Straining in pain, I welcomed the darkness as it took me.

## 2

# ICARUS

Fire roared at my back as I bent over the blade. Light indentations in the steel showed where I'd made earlier attempts, but nothing had been strong enough to work so far.

Sweating, I surrounded the sword with the wide clamp. Ultra-hard metals formed two points of contact, like a crab's claw with a pincer at the end and an additional spike inside. My fingers safely held the handle.

The sword clanged against the clamp and anvil where it lay. This had to work.

Months of selling trinkets at the market to earn enough for the next experiment, and the next, swept through my mind. The sword itself cost a month's wages. As it was, Father and I lived mostly on beans and vegetable greens and, when we could get it, a bit of cheese or crusty bread. At night, I only drank tea or coffee to trick myself into thinking I'd eaten.

I squeezed the handle.

"Work, work, work!" I commanded under my breath.

Shadows filled the dark smithy. My gaze shot up, but no one else was here. If war-torn Eriset knew what I trying to do…

The blade groaned. I held my breath, squeezing the handle harder. I'd added a new feature to this version of my invention—not only the double pinch points, but a way to make them vibrate when they reached a certain level of tension.

"A little more."

Grimacing and half-turning my face to the side in case the steel shattered, I forced more pressure on the blade. With a cry, muscles shaking and damp with sweat, I squeezed the clamp with all my strength.

*Crack!*

The blade split into three pieces.

I whooped and threw the clamp to the side. Heaving in air, I bent to look more closely at the sword. Yes, my materials were hard enough and positioned just the right way to break the steel. My invention worked! Two of the pieces of the blade lay like a puzzle on the anvil. The other lay on the ground.

A blade broken by human strength. This could change people's lives. I grinned at the shattered weapon.

Now if I could repeat the results, faster this time, in motion…

Reality crashed back in.

I couldn't afford another sword to use for an experiment. I'd already depleted our resources to get to this point. Helping at the smithy and selling simple machines at market weren't enough. It didn't help that buyers often commented that I was squandering my life by still living with my father and not finding a more stable profession. What business was it of theirs to assume they knew about my life?

But my experiment had *worked!* I knew it would. I knew it! This invention could save lives. It could protect people in the Labyrinth from raiding parties that sometimes came down from Eriset. Hell, maybe it could stop a war somewhere.

I ran a hand over my streaming face. I was getting ahead of myself. Carefully, I picked up the clamp where it lay on the stone pavement.

My device could change the world. I just needed to get it into the hands of someone who could help me.

At that idea, I scoffed. Father was a kind man, but not one with means. He'd lived in the Labyrinth his whole life and expected to stay here for what remained of it. To him, riches were a fantasy. Even moving south to more protected areas sounded far-fetched to him. He'd never go for it. The last time I'd made the suggestion, he said he'd miss the spiders here. He provided specimens to a second-rate university a few hours ride south. He loved naming plants and insects. For as long as I could remember, he tucked them into the many pockets on his clothes whenever he found them. Laundry day was a terror.

Rotating my wonderful device in the light of the fire, it seemed to wink at me. I'd given up friends and relationships to focus on this. Everyone said I was too obsessed. Wouldn't they be obsessed too if they thought they could create a hand-held device that could stop swords?

It was small enough to fit in my pack. A strange emptiness replaced the elation I'd felt a second ago. Now what? I needed more supplies to test it again and make it more effective. I needed a sponsor or patron to back its production. I had neither.

With a sigh, I toweled off my bare chest and slipped my brown shirt over my head. I had a world-changing invention in my bag—I was certain—but no way to get it to people in need.

"FATHER." I EASED OPEN THE DOOR. THE SMELL OF DRY wood and old pipe smoke greeted me like a friend. "I did it! My invention works!"

Father rose from the table, where he'd been fiddling with specimens. "Oh ho! Well done, my boy!" He clapped me on the back. None of the carefully reined criticism that sometimes shone through his eyes remained. Just pride and victory.

I beamed, shrugging off my pack and setting it against the table leg. Our front room consisted of a table, a stove, and a pile of clutter in the corner. Further back were our bedrooms. The house was tiny. But now, if I could get this defensive tool off the ground, we could sell the place and move into a much nicer one.

"The vibration made the difference," I explained.

Father snapped his fingers. "I should have suggested that. It's exactly what bird-eating plants use to sense prey is near."

I ignored the horrible mental image and settled into a chair. The wood groaned beneath me. This dining set existed since I was born, and the chairs fit me better when I was young. "It works. I still want to fiddle with it, get it smaller and working more consistently, but yes."

"I only have blowflies today," he replied, gesturing to the various small boxes and tubes on the table.

"You could go out and find more, couldn't you?" I felt bad as soon as I said it. My aging father shouldn't have to gather creatures to earn enough to support my inventions. Besides, it was easy to get lost on expeditions like his that strayed from the main roads. I needed to do it myself. "Never mind. I'll handle it."

Regret passed over Father's features. He started a kettle boiling. "I would, you know."

*Except that you won't move out of the Labyrinth.* It wasn't fair to think that way, but I was so close to success! Even searching for exotic spiders might pay off more in Kantharos or Zenia. Options were so limited here in northern Hyperion. Hell, even moving south would do us good. Hyperion was largely peaceful and prosperous, the notices said. I'd never been outside the Labyrinth, so I didn't know if moving farther from the war in Eriset would actually be better.

I suspected it would.

"I'm going to take a walk," I said suddenly, rising from the table. Maybe that would help me feel less tied down.

Father didn't protest. I didn't bring my bag along, just tromped out the door and down the path to the road. The path had three markers, each with a spider emblem, at intervals to prevent anyone getting lost. The Labyrinth suffered from bouts of enchanted smoke that drifted in from the north. Even without that, the trees here had a way of playing with your mind.

The main road ran past most of the residences. There wasn't a city center so much as a maze of interconnected paths and buildings. One public house served as the main hub for news and gossip. Most of the markets were hosted just outside it.

I slouched past, my mood dipping. What use was an invention if no one could use it? Now that I'd broken my only sword, adjustments to the design had to pause anyway. Would all that work really end with no mark in history? Maybe it was time to get a real job after all.

Murmured talking sounded from inside the pub. Night was falling, dusky and shadowy but not full dark. The sun was invisible. I approached the notice board tacked just inside the door.

*No, no, no.* I dismissed each notice as I read it. Rubbing my short beard, I closed my eyes. *I can't dismiss every opportunity. Father and I have to live. And I need a new blade for my work.*

I scanned the pieces of parchment again. Near the top, on white paper with clean edges, as if it had been sliced rather than ripped, was a notice for a palace attendant.

The palace? The Sun God's palace? We rarely got such notices this far north. I looked closer.

Good pay, simple duties, must live at the palace... Yes, there was the official golden seal. For a second, I considered taking the seal and popping it in my pocket for some quick money later.

This looked too good to be true.

All those interested were to go to the tax office on the southern end of the Labyrinth by tomorrow afternoon, packed to leave immediately.

*Tomorrow afternoon!* My heartbeat jogged. This was the chance I'd been waiting for. It was sudden but what better place to debut my invention than the palace? My device could help soldiers defend our people.

I tore the paper off the board and took it with me. Father would understand why I wanted to take a job so far away. Opportunities like this only arrived once in a lifetime.

Why did I think I would be the only one willing to pack everything for a chance to work at the palace?

The tax collector building practically burst with men and women carrying all their belongings on their back. I'd made sure to tuck my steel-breaking invention carefully between layers of clothes. When—if—I got to the palace, I wanted it to stay all in one piece.

A royal representative wearing a white and gold suit called each of us into the back room one by one. Since the paper hadn't specified what kinds of duties the job called for, I had no idea how to prepare. Not that I could have. I had my strength and determination to get the position. That was pretty much it.

"Icarus?" The royal representative read the name uncertainly from a list.

"That's me!" People made way for me so I could reach the front of the crowd. Gods, this room was hot. And I was about to speak to an emissary from King Lox himself. I ran a hand down my face as I followed him into the back room.

The door closed with a click. All other sounds muted.

The representative—a willowy, middle-aged man with thick curls similar to mine and soft hands that didn't look like mine at all—gestured for me to sit. I slung off my pack and sat.

"Name?"

My brows ticked downward. "Icarus." Didn't they already know that? He just read it off the sheet.

"Current occupation?"

I hesitated. "Smith." At least I helped out a few times a month.

"Family?"

"What?"

The man's eyes rose accusingly to mine. "Living family. What family do you have?"

"Oh. Father. I have my father, and that's it."

The man hummed and jotted something down. "Partner?"

"No."

"Willingness to serve the Sun God King Lox in whatever capacity he requires?"

"Yes," I said quickly.

"Patriotic, are you?"

Just yesterday, I'd considered moving to a different Realm, but I nodded anyway. Whatever it took to get to the palace. "I can lift anything, I'm good with machines and steel, I can—"

"Would your employer say you're loyal?"

An odd question, considering I wanted to leave the smithy for this new opportunity. "Yes. Definitely."

"Courageous?"

"Mm hm." I nodded, flat-lipped. Heaping praises on myself felt weird and arrogant. Surely they didn't want someone like that in the palace.

The representative made a final dot on the paper. "Very good. Wait outside." His expression told me nothing about how my interview had gone.

And his words had told me nothing about the kind of work I was signing up for.

Loyal? Brave? Did they need guards or soldiers? That sounded ridiculous, since they would need extra training. If King Lox were raising more people for the army, he wouldn't restrict the notice to only one person. The palace needed a single person from the Labyrinth. That was all.

I picked up my bag and left in a daze. Had I done well?

An hour passed. One by one, each of the others had their chance to answer the strange questions. I counted them as they went in and out. Finally, the last person had their turn. I stiffened. My stomach complained since I hadn't eaten all day, but I didn't care. There was food aplenty at the palace. I'd heard the palace was impossible to look at, bright as the sun, and inside there were meats and pies and sweets and everything one could want. My mouth watered and I swallowed.

The man in the white suit stepped out of the room, as he'd done many times, scanned his list, and looked up. None of the applicants said a word. Among us was a young mother with her child. There was a girl I recognized from a large family up the road from us, and the man who ran a milk service we couldn't afford to use.

My hand flexed over the canvas bag. I could barely feel the hard outline of my invention beneath the clothes.

"Icarus." He pronounced my name wrong, different from the first time, but he definitely meant me.

"Here!" I jumped up. "I'm ready."

The crowd around me scowled and wilted. One man openly groaned with disappointment and disbelief.

"It's an honor," the representative said without expression.

"Yes. Yes, it is." My face split into a smile. For once, life was going my way. Between my invention and this new job in Hyperion's palace, I felt like I could fly.

## ❧ 4 ❧

## ICARUS

I could look at King Lox's palace without burning my
eyes, but it was still taller and more magnificent than I
could have invented in my mind. It was white and gold—
that part was true. An enormous sunburst was painted in the
center of the façade, with giant rays pointing out in all
directions.

The grounds were even better, probably teeming with rare
insects and spiders. I didn't go looking. Lush plants lined clear
walkways. At every intersection stood a yellow sign pointing to
a library or the musician's dome. It was a dream. I even saw a
goldsmith on site. Maybe I'd work there.

The royal representative, who'd ridden a pure white horse
most of the way that made me feel like some grubby child
riding next to them, continued moving closer to the palace
itself.

In the palace, the notice had said. I had a job in that
palace.

I didn't get lucky like this. Humans from the Labyrinth didn't get offers to serve a god for untold sums of money.

It was almost suspicious.

We reached milk-white doors twice as tall as I was, and the royal representative finally spoke. "Listen carefully to every instruction. Do not deviate. I will fetch a trainer for you."

I nodded.

He disappeared through the doors. A moment later, he returned with a small female. She rose only to my waist and had leaves in place of hair. She wore brown bark-like patches on her skin—obviously a god or demi-god. The man in the suit struck me as human, but this person clearly wasn't.

"Hello, um, my lady," I said. Lord and lady were standard ways to address the deathless. A safe bet since I didn't know her name or rank. Much higher than me, that was for sure.

"This is Icarus," said the representative. "He's here as the new assistant to Ray Sixteen."

The bark woman regarded me shrewdly. "Come." She didn't tell me her name.

I followed her, leaving the white-suited man behind, through the double doors. This wasn't the main entrance, I noticed right away. That made sense, of course. I doubted I had a high-profile job here, but I hadn't expected an opulent marble hall with high ceilings and music playing. Besides the two of us, no one else was here. This might not be the main entrance, but it felt fit for a king. I gripped the strap of my bag tighter.

"You will sleep in an adjoining room," the deathless woman began in a clipped voice. "Every morning and evening, you will serve the ray his meal. You will bathe him.

You will clean for him. You will keep him in a state and form worthy of the Sun God. You will assist him with his every need. You will address him as 'my excellent ray, the Sun God's favorite.'"

My mind scrambled to keep up. Excellent ray? Bathe him?

"If King Lox calls for him, you will escort him to his meeting. If King Lox visits the ray's chamber, you will bow with your face to the ground unless my king releases you."

I wished I could write this down. The notice said the work would be easy, but this was a lot to remember.

The deathless woman halted beside a patch of smooth bright wall. "Icarus, is it?"

"Yes." In the sudden pause, I realized my breaths came shorter than usual.

"Whatever you do, do not touch the Sun God's favorite."

My mouth formed half a question but the bark woman was already pulling a key from a small pouch at her side. She inserted it into a practically invisible keyhole, and turned.

The door was a miracle. Set straight into the wall, it opened without sound. Closed, it was utterly hidden unless you knew where to find it. I'd have to figure out how it was made.

The deathless woman ushered me inside. Curtains smelling of moss and lightning storms blocked our way. I offered to hold them to the side so we could continue.

Everything here was deep red and heady with scent. My head swam.

"Hello!"

On one side of the large room—maybe a bedchamber for a god?—sat the most beautiful man I'd ever seen. His leg stretched out oddly in front of him, as if it was broken. But his face. And his body. And his *everything*...

I stood totally still.

Honey-brown curls sat short but full on his head, framing brown eyes set deep. His expression was more open than I'd seen in any adult, and he clearly was an adult. Maybe a couple years younger than me. Or—what was I thinking?—he had to be a god, and they didn't age the same way. His full mouth curled in a dimpled smile to see me.

Me. Scruffy, backwoods me.

His skin was flawless. Not a scratch on him, except for the leg. His neck formed a smooth stretch over his adam's apple to the line of his collarbone. Because he only wore a short, brown skirt or something, I got a clear view of the artistic sweep of his chest and abs.

Wow.

I couldn't remember the last time I'd reacted like this to anyone.

"Hello," he said again. "Are you my new assistant?"

I glanced at the bark woman to be sure. She gave a single curt nod.

"Yes," I affirmed, tongue heavy and dry.

*Stop staring at him like he's dinner. Shit.*

I cleared my throat. "Yes, I am."

A shadow of apprehension crossed the young man's features, there then gone. "Good. I'm Jacin."

*Jacin.* Hadn't the others called him Ray or something?

"I'm Icarus. I'm glad I can serve you, my lord."

Jacin's hands flexed on the arms of his chair like he wanted to rise. I started moving forward to help, but stopped myself when he visibly tensed. The deathless woman had been deadly serious when she told me not to touch him.

Did people often touch Jacin when he didn't want them to? The thought made rage rise to the back of my throat. I knew almost nothing about him, but it was clear he was precious.

"Do you require assistance?" asked the bark woman.

"No, no. I'm all right," said Jacin, slumping back down. Disappointment painted his features.

I raised a hand. "I can—"

"No!" Jacin jabbed a finger in my direction, pinning me in place. "Stay there. I can get to bed myself."

I shot a glance behind me and found what he referred to.

*Oh fuck me.*

I needed to jettison these lustful thoughts fast. There were more important things than indulging this unexpected attraction, like finding someone to review my invention.

The bed was dark red, softer looking than any I'd slept in, deep with pillows. Two baskets sat on the floor near it. Food? Drink? No. I spied a suspiciously phallic-shaped object poking out among various oils and creams.

I turned back to Jacin. His beauty was otherworldly.

And it finally made sense.

Jacin was a consort to the King.

## 5

# JACIN

I shifted uncomfortably in my chair, my splinted leg screaming. For now, I'd stay put. Besides, talking to my new assistant sounded more interesting than going to bed. I'd slept a lot this past week anyway.

Icarus seemed nice. At least he looked me in the eye.

"If there's nothing else you require," Laurel prompted, folding her bark-covered hands.

"No. I don't need anything," I said with a smile.

She didn't smile back. She probably knew what I'd done to Roshan. My excitement about the new assistant dimmed a little.

With a bow, she left.

Icarus remained behind, clutching the strap of a dirty bag slung over his shoulder. It looked heavy.

"Do you want to put that down?" I asked, scanning the room for a good place. My chamber was supposed to be ready for King Lox at any time, and that meant being clean. When I didn't find a good spot, I grimaced an apology. "There's a room just through there where you can stay." I pointed to a small door at the far corner. Too bad he couldn't find a place here to relax, so we could get to know each other.

"Thank you, my... excellent ray of the Sun God's..."

I laughed.

"The favorite," he finished, red as the curtains. For such a strong-looking man, he didn't look relaxed at all. "I'm sorry. I'll learn it, my lord." He dipped his head.

"That's okay. I'm not mad."

"I promise I'll do my best."

"I believe you."

He raised his eyes. Again, his scarred fingers flexed around the strap of his bag. I doubted a minotaur could pry it from him.

"Why don't you set down your things and join me... there?" I pointed to a chair upholstered with burnt orange fabric across the room. No sense taking extra risks.

"Of course, my lord."

"Jacin's fine. I like it when people call me Jacin." Well, I'd enjoyed it in the burning moments before my leg brushed Roshan. Before that, no one ever took me up on calling me by my real name. It was an honor, I supposed, to only hear my honorific, but it left me feeling a little distant.

Icarus's lips twitched. "I'll call you Jacin if you want me to."

"I do." Happiness bubbled up at his pronouncement.

"Right through here?" He indicated the small door. Could he fit through it all right? I always thought it looked too short for me, but then, I was taller than most humans I knew.

He turned the handle and went inside. His hair scraped the door frame, but otherwise it was fine.

I exhaled. That room was a small space to offer him, but I was subject to the King and his gifts. Icarus was a gift sent to help me.

I tried to lean back in my chair, but my bad leg spasmed at the movement. My back arched and lungs seized as I waited for the sensation to pass. *One, two, three...* The stabbing pain lessened to a throbbing ache.

Icarus emerged in a flash. I thought he'd stay in there at least long enough to clean up. Dirt smudged his lightly bearded face and a faint splash of mud stained his trousers. His simple brown and tan outfit wasn't made of the fine material I was used to. But something about him drew me in. Maybe the realness. Moments ago, he'd walked under the sunlight outside the palace.

Longing plagued my chest a moment before clearing. I had all the sunlight I needed from my king.

"Sit," I said. "Please."

Icarus obeyed. Even though he still seemed uneasy, he spread out in the chair, resting his muscular forearms on the sides and spreading his legs.

"So," I began. "Icarus. Where are you from?"

"The Labyrinth."

My eyebrows shot up. "Where's that?"

"The... In northern Hyperion, near the Bridge."

Had I said something wrong? He acted surprised I didn't know. I swallowed down any sense of embarrassment. "Ah. Were you a personal assistant there?"

His eyes sparkled and lips twisted with amusement. "No. I was a smith. A metal worker."

He did have the look of someone who'd done some hard

labor. "Oh, that's interesting!" I tried resettling my leg in its splint, but nothing felt right. It stuck out like a useless pillar.

"Can I get you something to make you more comfortable?"

My gaze shot up again. Icarus's eyes were wide with the question. "No," I said. "The healers give me potions every day so I can get strong again." Guilt gnawed at my mind. Not only had I caused Roshan's death, but I hadn't done my exercises in a week. My body had already become softer, but, after my short visit to the King's chamber, I barely wanted to get out of bed. The gap of time without an assistant was extra difficult. I only managed one bath, and that came with lots of grunting and cursing.

I tried not to look at my broken leg, but it drew my eye over and over again. The Sun King was immortal. What if he didn't want to wait for me and found a new favorite?

"If I may ask," Icarus began carefully, "is the entire leg in pain?"

No sense in lying. "Yes. But I'll become strong again. The lower part is broken." I bit my lip. Icarus treated me kindly and spoke to me almost like a friend. He couldn't know what happened to my last assistant. It was only an accident, my clumsiness. I never wanted Roshan to die.

Icarus scanned from my face to my leg. "So your knee isn't the problem?"

I shook my head.

A smile ghosted over his features as he considered my splint. "I could—if you want, if you command—make a hinge for you, something that would be more comfortable, so you can bend your leg."

I gripped the armrests and leaned forward. A spike of pain

shot from my calf to my hip, but I ignored it. "You can do that?"

"Yes, it would be no trouble at all. If you point the way to a shop with the materials. Gold is soft, but I remember seeing a goldsmith on the way here...?"

There was a goldsmithing workshop nearby? "That would be the King's decision." I doubted he'd allow a golden splint. Especially after everything.

"Of course. Other metals would work just as well." His hands clasped and unclasped in his lap, apparently eager to get started.

I beamed. This Icarus had nice, earnest eyes. If the King provided me with someone so helpful and friendly, there was a chance I remained his favorite after all.

# 6

## ICARUS

The next day, I managed to get the tools I needed from a servant who delivered dinner, which was oysters with some kind of red spice on them, pomegranate seeds, and grape-leaf-wrapped figs for Jacin. I got a much simpler potato and carrot pie with gravy. Thank goodness I didn't have to find the kitchen on my own in this enormous place. Their pantry alone must have been huge to create such different meals.

When I told the server I had to fix something in the room, she returned a few minutes later with the simple objects I needed: flexible straps, an assortment of pegs and screws, and a small hammer. I needed a blade too, but she told me weapons weren't allowed.

Made sense.

Good thing I had a clamp to break steel. I originally made it to shatter weapons, but if I beat the splint thin enough along particular lines, my invention could do the rest of the work.

Jacin's splint looked clumsy and painful, jutting his leg

straight out, holding the entire thing rigid from his hip to his foot. It was little more than a board with straps tightened over the top.

When I talked to him yesterday, I eventually noticed angry red lacerations and bruises all over his shin. Some of the skin looked mangled deeply enough to scar.

It took me awhile to look away from the rest of him, like a fool. Of course *a consort of the King* fit together like the most perfect machine. There was no need to keep ogling him.

Right now, though, looking away was really fucking hard.

"Step back." Jacin held out a hand. "I don't want you to do it. Just check the water."

He sat in the same chair as before—surely there were more comfortable ones in the palace for someone with a broken leg —eyes tightly shut as he bent over to untie the splint.

"I'm happy to help."

"No! The water," he said sharply, with no arrogance or meanness. Only command.

I bit my tongue to keep from saying anything else. What was so wrong about saving him a little pain? It would take me five seconds to undo the laces and free his leg. I wouldn't even need to touch him, since that was such a big deal.

The tub sank into the floor on the other end of the large platform. Water poured out from dual spigots—one hot, the other cold. I tested the temperature with my hand. Soaking warm. I would have loved having something like this to wash off after a long day. At least a small private washroom was provided in my living quarters. Nothing like this luxurious bath, but enough to get clean. The very fact it felt cramped reminded me of home. I could see getting used to it.

"The temperature feels good," I reported. "Do you want it a particular way?"

"Just hot enough to sting your hand, please."

I adjusted the spigots so more boiling hot water ran out. Steam rose from the large round tub. It was big enough that two steps led down into it.

I glanced up. Jacin's bare back moved erratically as he struggled to remove the splint.

*Don't jump up and help. He's in charge here and told you not to.*

After far too long, the terrible splint dropped to the floor. Jacin heaved a deep breath and straightened, his chin tipping up.

Gods, he was beautiful.

"Icarus."

I stood.

"Don't come any closer. Stay there. My king likes moss and orange blossom. Mix them into the water." He didn't twist to look at me. How was he going to get into the bath if I couldn't help him?

I looked around for moss and orange blossom—odd, I thought—but didn't see any. "Where are they?"

"Scented oils. They're near the tub."

That made more sense than shoveling moss into a bath. I found the basket he referred to and lifted out each labeled bottle: "Salt for smooth skin", "Wax for lips", "Cream for soft hair", "Fine oil for the King's play", and finally "Orange blossom—for hair" and "Moss—for body."

The King's play? My neck heated as I realized what that one was for. I checked the contents of the bottle. It was still sealed, oil rising to the lid. Someone must have brought a new one recently. How often did the Sun King come here? I couldn't believe I hadn't thought about it before. The god himself—King of Hyperion—lived in this palace. Just last month citizens of the Labyrinth had hosted its yearly Festival of the Longest Day. Father and I had caught the end of it.

Jacin was that god's consort. Maybe he visited this room all the time.

The idea made me buzz with the sheer importance of what I'd been asked to do.

I poured some of the scented oil into the water and swirled it with my hand. It smelled much better than I would have expected. I inhaled deeply and set the orange blossom and moss bottles at the edge of the bath. "Do you want any of the other things here?"

"No, just those two."

Jacin was pushing himself to stand. And he was completely naked.

I sucked in a breath. This was normal. Totally normal. I was his assistant. He was taking a bath and... normal.

But it didn't feel that way.

Jacin rotated, his shattered leg dangling at his side, bloody and bruised. Even broken, he stole my breath. He was tall and magnificent and muscular, sculpted out of strength and softness. If I were the King, I'd come here every night. I'd bring Jacin to wherever I had my god bedroom and, as long as Jacin wanted it too, I'd dote on him.

*Stop daydreaming about this man while he's obviously suffering.*

Was *he* used to this—being naked in front of his assistants? Stupid question. Of course he was. He showed no self-consciousness (why should he, with a body like that?), only pain.

I hated how much pain Jacin was in. This was the palace! Did they not have something he could take to ease it?

He used the chair to hop closer to the tub.

"Move," he gritted out.

Stung, I walked backward down the stairs to maintain distance. The growled word didn't sound annoyed at me, but it still hurt to be dismissed like that when all I wanted to do was help.

For money.

For my invention.

Not for fantasizing like some teenager.

I cleared my throat and made a wide arc around him to retrieve the fallen splint. "If I can help in any way, just let me know."

He nodded, tight.

"Can I pick this up?" I asked, pointing. Jacin was so particular about me not getting near him that the rule might apply to things that he had previously touched.

"Fine." Jacin limped, shaking, into the hot bath water. As he lowered himself in, letting water lap over his thighs, his hips, his torso, his face contracted into an expression of orgasm. His mouth opened wide, eyes shut, neck straining.

My cock twitched and hardened at the sight. Apparently, the years I spent choosing work over sex or relationships had made me a godsdamned pervert.

"Is the King visiting tonight?" I asked, voice husky and low.

Jacin didn't open his eyes, but his face relaxed as the bath soothed his poor body. "My king hasn't visited yet."

*Yet?* "You mean, he hasn't come here?" I picked up the heavy splint. No reason it should be so bulky and large.

"Um..." Jacin squinted open an eye. "I need to be ready for him at all times."

I frowned. How had the King not visited Jacin? Wasn't Jacin his consort? This entire room was clearly meant for... certain activities. I didn't name them to myself, so as not to excite my overeager cock.

"It'll probably take me an hour to adjust your sling. Is that all right?"

He waved a languorous hand. He looked halfway to sleep. The tense lines around his eyes and mouth had faded, and he looked younger. "That's fine."

"I'll be out as soon as I can."

"That sounds good."

I turned to retreat into my room.

"Icarus." He said my name mussed and sleepy.

"Yes?"

"Thank you."

# 7

# ICARUS

I flexed the new moveable splint back and forth. The hinges didn't make a sound. Not only that, but my clamp had worked perfectly once I weakened the metal along the lines I wanted. Now the splint was shorter so it wouldn't jab into Jacin's hip or groin, and he could move his knee.

Someone at the palace had to see the value of what I'd made. It was good not only for defense but also for metalworking like this. Grim satisfaction played across my face. Maybe today I could meet a few new people, see who I needed to talk to.

Honestly, I was grateful the Sun King wasn't visiting Jacin today. I'd barely gotten a grasp on what I was supposed to be doing here. Falling on my face before the King sounded like too much to take in at once. Besides, what if I had to stay like that while the King and Jacin...

No. No more thoughts like that. It wasn't my business. My business was to assist Jacin with whatever he needed while figuring out a way to get my invention into the hands of the right people. Simple and lucrative.

I held the new splint in one hand and pushed the door back out into Jacin's chamber. It was perfectly quiet—no music like there had been just outside in the hall. Steam curled above the bath. Jacin's head fell back against the tiles that bordered the tub.

He didn't look conscious.

"My lord," I said. "Jacin?"

He sniffed and raised his head. A guileless smile stretched his perfect mouth. "Is it done?" He raised his arms high, flexing and yawning.

I looked away, down at the new splint. "Yes. When you're ready, you can try it on."

He stood, his pain obviously reduced compared to what it was before, and cast around for something to help him get out of the water.

Was it so bad for me to offer my shoulder as support? But I didn't say that. He'd reject my help immediately.

"Here," I said, dragging over the chair.

"Stop!" His eyes formed circles. Not anger but fear. Fear large enough to make him forget his pain and hop out on hands and his good leg. Water dripped over his chest, down to his generous cock. The tips of his hair near his nape formed little points that made rivulets run down his back. For what felt like the dozenth time, I was struck speechless.

Jacin waved his hand to make me move. I set the new splint beside the chair so he could put it on himself and retreated several steps away.

He didn't bother to put on clothes. Instead, he struggled

forward toward the chair until he could settle into it. Sighing, he took a moment to compose himself.

"I'm covered in wrinkles," he said regretfully, as if he should be ashamed of something.

I laughed before I could stop myself.

He cast me a curious look. "Look," he said, holding up a pruny hand. "My feet are the same."

"It's just from the water."

"It'll pass soon."

I almost pointed out that it didn't matter—in general and especially because the Sun King apparently had no intention of stopping by to see him.

Jacin lifted the splint. "It's shorter."

"Yes," I said, smiling. "This way, it should let you move a little. If you fasten that bit around your knee... there, yes... then it doesn't need to go all the way up your leg. See, it can bend!" I hinged my hand to demonstrate.

It took Jacin considerably less time to fasten the improved version to his leg than it had taken him to remove the last one. A hot bath had done wonders. And, I liked to think, my new design helped too.

He slowly raised his straightened knee up. Amazement lit his face. Back and forth, he moved his leg.

I grinned at him.

He grinned back, eyes glossy. It made me want to create more simple things for him. This hadn't been difficult, and it obviously meant so much.

"This is wonderful!"

"Are you more comfortable?"

"Much more." He sat straight in the chair, both knees bent.

Apart from the contraption strapped to his leg, he could have been uninjured. "Look!"

"I see."

"You're a very kind person, Icarus."

More often, I was called distant, obsessive, focused, quiet. Not kind. But I wore the new word like a medal. My whole body warmed with the compliment.

"It wasn't difficult. I was happy to do it," I muttered. "I'm sure you have smiths at the palace who could do it for you too. I was just here." What was I blathering about? I forced myself to stop talking.

"I don't think anyone else would do this for me. Unless the King made a special exception," he added.

"Really? What if you need to walk somewhere?"

"I always stay in this room."

I stared. "Always? You never leave?" I softened my tone. I didn't mean to sound accusatory, but the questions came out harsh with surprise. "What about when you visit the Sun King?" He may never have come here, but Jacin must visit him with some frequency.

Jacin's carved lips drew into a line and his eyes darted downward. "My king is very important and busy." He hinged his knee again, testing out the new movement.

*I shouldn't ask, shouldn't ask, shouldn't ask...*

"You... have visited him before, haven't you?"

Jacin's gaze flitted up to mine before dropping again. "Oh! Um... once. You ask a lot of questions."

"I'm sorry."

"I like your questions. You can ask them."

My guts flipped. Jacin looked more steadily back at me

now. What was life like for him, that he stayed cooped in this, frankly, erotic room where no one visited? It had to be lonely.

When was the last time anyone had touched him, even innocently?

"What happened to your leg?" The question was out before I could censor it.

Jacin's expression clouded, golden cheeks turning red. "An accident."

After a moment of quiet, I realized he wouldn't say more. Tension floated through the scented air. If someone had painted the scene, Jacin would have looked like a young king sitting on that raised chair, looking down at me. But he was too open, too sweet even, to fit that profile.

"Do you like it here?" I tried. "It's..." I searched for a word. "Grand."

He shook his head yes. "It's nicer now that you're here."

I loved the way he threw compliments out like raining coins. Like it was the most natural thing because he was so rich with them. It made me want to revel in them and give them back.

"I'm glad I was chosen. The King is lucky to have you by his side."

Jacin blushed.

"I'm going to drain the bath," I said quickly. *And stop getting wrapped up in his charm.*

He watched me work, idly bending his knee, apparently in no pain at all.

## ❦ 8 ❦

## JACIN

The Guardian always arrived in the morning.

I was usually happy to see her, even though she never smiled. Now, though, after embarrassing myself and dooming Roshan in the King's bedroom, I dreaded her knock.

Leaning back against the headboard, I chewed my hard-boiled egg, but it tasted like nothing. Nothing was still better than the vial of green goop the healers added to my tray. But both would make me strong again.

My bed was much softer than the chair. After a week with me, Icarus knew to keep his distance, so it didn't feel so vulnerable being on the lower parts of my room. Besides, now I could go up and down the steps. I still had to move slowly, but Icarus's invention made it possible for me to limp using both legs.

Several paces away, he sat, shoving bacon and steamed pudding into his mouth. Roshan never ate in front of me, so I didn't think about whether our meals were different. I used to assume mine were finer, to match the favorite of the King, but Icarus's food looked more delicious. Maybe I just got that impression from the way he gobbled it up with such relish.

I finished my egg and scooted myself up. The back of the lightweight tunic I wore got trapped underneath me and I had to free it to straighten. Candles flickered on the end table by the bed.

"Icarus."

He raised his eyes from his plate, mouth full. He chewed furiously.

"Would you ask the person who brings the food if I could try one of your meals sometime?"

He finished chewing and swallowed. "You can try some of mine now if you want to."

"No." That wouldn't do. There was a reason the King offered me different food. I had to ask permission first. Also, traces of Icarus's spit were probably on his breakfast plate now. I couldn't put that into me. Doing so was probably at least as bad as brushing someone's hair with my leg. It might look like we'd kissed or something.

My neck heated at the mere idea. I'd never betray my king like that.

"Okay. I'll ask them. Is there—"

A knock sounded at the door.

Icarus's brow furrowed.

"That'll be the Guardian," I explained. "She comes every other day to check on me." At least she *did*. I had no idea why she'd stayed away so long this time.

Icarus's face lightened, and he set his food to the side to answer the door.

*I haven't done anything wrong,* I reminded myself. The new splint didn't break any rules, did it? Icarus hadn't touched me to secure it or anything.

My stomach tightened so forcefully I felt the egg-like sickness inside me.

Sharp-eyed and heavily covered in cloaks, the Guardian entered. She towered over Icarus. I didn't know her true shape or nature, only that her eyes glowed yellow—not the soft golden glow of the Sun God but the piercing yellow of a black cat. She wore gloves and heavy boots, and her words were always the same.

"Good morning," I greeted.

Maybe this time she would lower her hood so I could see what she looked like. Maybe she'd stay longer than a few seconds.

"Rise and approach, most excellent ray."

Creakily, I did. The Guardian never reached out, never did anything except observe and sense if I had any contact with others since I'd seen her last.

Would my broken leg change that? Would she be able to tell that I hadn't touched anyone since the incident?

I stopped, still a few paces away from her. Icarus stood farther back, near the door, observing. Could the Guardian tell Icarus hadn't touched me, or would my injury mess with her senses?

"Closer," she demanded.

It was like I'd turned to stone. I couldn't move.

After a couple seconds, which probably made me look guilty all over again, she strode forward two paces until she stood right in front of me. She breathed slowly twice as her cat-like eyes looked me over.

Finally, she stepped back. "You have remained loyal to our king, the Sun God."

I exhaled.

"He requires an audience with you."

My heart stopped. "The King does?" I yearned to ask the reason, but I held my tongue.

"Yes. Have your assistant bring you there this evening."

Without waiting for a response, she turned on her heel and left through the door Icarus held open for her.

I sank down on the foot of the bed. Had the King forgiven me? Did he think I'd learned all I needed to know when I observed him a week ago? Was he going to execute me for causing such a scene in his bedchamber?

My heart ricocheted against my ribs.

Yesterday, I bathed in orange blossom water. That was good. I had more movement in my leg, so if I had to kneel...

"Breathe, Jacin."

My attention shot to Icarus, who stood a respectful distance in front of me, holding out both hands as if he wished he could do more to help.

"Breathe."

I took a shaky breath, vision swimming. "The King... wants me." I hadn't realized how afraid I was that he would abandon me until I heard the summons.

"Of course he does. Keep breathing."

I tried.

"Are you... excited?" Icarus asked, strangely unsure.

"Yes. Yes, I am."

"It's..." He swallowed hard. "It's natural to be nervous. This is exciting, right?"

I nodded vigorously. "Yes, it's what I've wanted." Icarus didn't know how my leg got broken, and I didn't want to make him afraid to come with me. I could be afraid for both of us.

"You... Have you... done this before?" he asked. His voice sounded odd and strained.

"I've watched."

Icarus blinked a few times. "So you know what to do?"

Visions of bodies everywhere, of sucking and kissing and thrusting and caressing, filled my mind. If only I knew which one to be, or if we'd be by ourselves. What would I do then? "I think so."

"Well, good," he said gruffly.

I blew out another slow, steadying breath. Icarus was right. This development was exciting. Perhaps the King finally wanted me under those lights with him. I'd been promised this encounter since I was eighteen.

"Before we go," I said, "you need to paint me gold. I'm sure we can find some long paintbrushes..."

I trailed off when I saw the look on Icarus's face. Something vaguely like horror.

I chuckled. "Just solid gold. You don't need to be an artist, although I think you probably are one." I held out my splinted leg. My laughter faded. "I'm sorry you need to get close to me. I promise to stay still and not move." *Even when you get to my foot.*

"That's not... That's fine. I'm happy to serve you in any way." Something lurked beneath his words, but I didn't press. I'd be nervous too in his position.

Shit, I was nervous in mine.

# 9

# ICARUS

I'd almost gotten used to life with Jacin. The days made more sense now. There was a pattern to the cleaning and serving and laying out whatever he needed. We talked pretty freely with each other. I could hardly believe it—a consort of the Sun God himself had become my... Well, why didn't I say it? We were friends.

The money didn't hurt either. Yesterday, my first payment arrived. More than Father made in five trips to the university, and I'd earned it in a week. Keeping a few coins back for myself, I sent the rest to him. Hopefully he didn't miss me too much. He could get sentimental.

And the work was light, at least compared to what I was used to. The food was hearty, the bed comfortable, the company always good. The steel-breaking clamp lived in the back of my mind, but I hadn't found the right moment to show somebody.

Today, though, could change that.

Jacin and I would visit the King. I decided not to bring my

invention on this trip. It was nerve-racking enough meeting the deity the entire kingdom worshipped. I'd never been very religious myself, but I tipped musicians when I could and I knew the main poems for festivals. This time, I would observe and learn everything I could. Hopefully make a good impression.

I chose a suit of dark blue with yellow accents—the nicest one I owned—and I still felt shabby. My shoes had stains on them and my hair decided to curl in odd directions this morning.

Sighing, I turned away from the little circular mirror in the corner. What did it matter? The King wouldn't spare me a glance with Jacin in the room. I kicked the bag with my invention carefully under my bed. Next time.

When I exited into Jacin's chamber, I stopped short. He stood in the middle of the room, stark naked again. He had to stop doing that. It was enough to burst someone's heart (or balls).

The splint lay beside him. I realized he was holding something out to me.

I lifted an eyebrow, suddenly surly. "What's that?"

"I told you. It's the gold paint. I requested extra-long brushes."

Despite trying to resist, my traitorous eyes dipped down. I'd never seen anyone so at ease in his body as Jacin. It was as if he had no idea he was beautiful enough to start wars.

"They said this was all they could do," he added apologetically. He held the paintbrush—it looked like a thin rod, long enough to buckle slightly in the middle—by its bristles.

I approached him slowly, like I would a barn cat I didn't

want to scare away. Jacin had made it clear plenty of times that he didn't like the idea of me getting close to him at all. His throat bobbed uncomfortably as I drew nearer. Reaching out, I took the other end of the paintbrush.

"Gold paint's there," he said, indicating a pot filled with what looked like actual liquid gold. "It dries fast, but I need to be covered before I see the King."

Covered. The word echoed uselessly in my mind as if I'd never encountered the concept before. Covered?

"I'll stay very still," he said, looking straight ahead. "Just... do your best not to brush up against me or touch me. Please. Please."

This was getting ridiculous. I didn't intend on ravishing him. Who would even know if I accidentally grazed him with a knuckle while following the King's command?

But Jacin's eyes pleaded with me to listen, so I would.

I took another step forward, an arm's length from him now. I'd never stood so close. Gods, he even smelled good.

Distracting myself from the way my dick perked up, I dipped the brush in paint. "Is there a right way to do this?"

"You can start anywhere."

Mouth dry, I reached out with the brush, trying to maintain the distance he wanted. "How about here?" I aimed the bristles at his shoulder, where it swelled down to his arm.

"That's fine."

Keeping my fingers on the very end of the brush to create the largest distance, I drew a thick, golden line across Jacin's skin. Excess paint dripped down the side of his pec, like he'd been dipped in gold.

I wasn't going to make it. Desperation fueled my movements as I moved that absurdly flaccid paintbrush over the rest of Jacin's shoulder. I wasn't exact. The brush flopped all over the place. At one point, I accidentally flicked his face, creating golden freckles across his nose. He laughed, although I could tell he stood a little too rigid. Maybe he was just afraid I'd touch him, or maybe he was worried about his meeting with the King.

I didn't like the way he seized up after hearing the summons. Shouldn't he be relieved and glad to be summoned to the King's side?

Hard to be relieved if you barely knew someone.

Jacin talked about the King like a subject, not a lover. And he'd definitely been anxious to see him. Why was King Lox keeping Jacin here like a pet to be used whenever he felt like it and ignored the rest of the time? Jacin was doing everything he could to please him from afar, and, as far as I could tell, the King didn't give a shit about him.

Maybe that went too far. The gods had their own lives separate from humans. They thought differently. But still... Anger roiled inside me at the idea that Jacin had been left on his own, kept in limbo, and not even allowed to leave his room.

"Hey!"

I blinked.

"You've already done that part twice. I don't want to run out of paint." Jacin gave me a confused little smirk.

It was true. I'd painted his left shoulder and the left side of his torso twice over. I moved onto his arm, painting in strokes as smooth as I could muster with this absurdly long-handled brush.

When I reached his hand, Jacin held it out so I could get

between the fingers. It was delicate work, and I couldn't get all the crevices unless I slid my own fingers further down the brush for more control. He didn't shy away when I did that, so I kept my hand where it was. The adjustment made it so much easier to paint in details.

I did the same thing over his right side.

"Do the face next," he ordered. "I don't want it to be last." He lifted his chin so I could get better access to his neck.

It was a smooth column so beautiful and alive I could have pressed my lips to his pulse.

I shook my head. Back in the Labyrinth, I wasn't this horny. I needed to snap out of it. But then again, no one in the Labyrinth looked like Jacin.

"Keep going," he said, a hint of amusement dimpling his face. "I know it takes a long time."

*I don't mind. I'd do it for hours.*

I cursed myself for the thought and attempted to think of him like an actual statue. Difficult, considering his chest rose and fell with breathing and he kept watching me as I worked.

By the time I finished with his neck, my hand had inched up the brush again. I still kept far away enough that I didn't fear touching him, but the heat from his body soaked into my hand.

"Face down," I muttered. "You're taller than me."

He lowered his face and closed his eyes. This was more trust than he'd ever shown. I stood close enough to breathe against his skin and his eyes were shut. My insides writhed. I felt the heat of my own breath as it played across his cheekbones.

This was dangerous. And stupid. Incredibly stupid.

I indulged in one more shared breath while his slightly parted lips were close to mine.

Then I backed up. Jacin was going to see the Sun God today, for fuck's sake. I couldn't muck around playing pretend about something that would never happen. I wouldn't be another person treating Jacin like a prize instead of a man.

Clutching the far end of the paintbrush again, I covered the rest of his face, sloppier this time. It didn't feel like writing the truth on his skin when I did it this way.

Jacin's eyes fluttered open. For a second, when his gaze locked on mine, I thought he suspected that I'd fantasized about him, but then we both looked away.

Attraction was not a good enough reason to throw away a job that paid well and provided connections that could help me change the world.

Strengthened by that thought, I rushed through Jacin's toned back. It was impossible to find a corner of him that didn't exude effortless sex appeal, but I acted as quickly and as coldly as I could.

Jacin's legs had started to shake by the time I started on them. He held all his weight on one foot. I should have worked faster.

*Selfish bastard*, I scolded myself.

Lower back.

Ass.

Leg one.

On my knees, I began working on his injured leg. The damage turned his shin and calf into a mottled red map of the Realms. Ugly yellow-green bruises scored up the length of his lower leg.

I could work faster if I had more control over the brush, so I moved my hand down toward the soaking gold bristles again and moved my face closer. His leg trembled as I worked light and quick over the skin. I had the urge to mark every place where he'd been damaged to pay homage to his pain, but, for his sake, I didn't linger. The gold paint covered almost all evidence that he'd been hurt. For some reason, that bothered me.

"Okay?" I asked.

"I'm okay," he whispered.

I chanced a look up. He held his whole body tense enough to snap.

"I'm almost done," I assured him, working up his thigh now. It was muscular and perfect and unfair that I had to look at it.

The only thing left was...

"Everything?" I confirmed, my tone curt. My own legs had gone numb from kneeling.

"Yes."

I tapped my finger on the brush a few times. Dipped it in the paint. Drew in a breath.

*Just painting. Only painting.*

But it wasn't. Painting his cock was more intimate than any actual sex I'd had in my life. My heart thumped in my throat as I lowered the brush to his head.

A tiny inhalation of breath.

*Fuck me.*

I made small strokes all the way around the end, then light ones reaching higher. He started to thicken. I ignored the way he was growing. Besides, it didn't matter. If someone stroked my dick, I'd probably get hard too.

Like I was now. Achingly hard.

I painted faster, all the way up the shaft. It felt like a race. I'd be safe if I got to the end, then his balls wouldn't be in my face and I could stand and we could pretend this never happened. An ordinary day.

I huffed out a pained laugh.

Jacin twitched.

He was sensitive. Oh gods.

"Um, lift, please," I said hoarsely.

He gripped himself so I could reach the underside and balls and *why were there so many creases?*

Finally, I backed away, rising on prickling legs. I felt hot as an oven. The paintbrush clattered into the empty pot of gold, the shaft of the brush tall enough to tip it over.

Jacin looked like a god, different but beautiful. His expression was... insecure?

"The god won't be able to resist," I quipped. My attempt at lightness failed miserably. Did that sound like I was coming onto him? How could it not? I'd just painted his entire dick. I felt about to pass out. I must have been holding my breath.

Jacin was still rigid. Hopefully he couldn't tell I'd surpassed him there. I could hardly move without teasing my own sensitive cock on the seam of my pants.

"It's... natural," I said, when Jacin stayed silent. "A normal, natural reaction. It'll go back down in a bit."

I had to sit down. I really was going to pass out. Or, better yet, I needed some time alone in my little room to work out all this tension vibrating my bones, and then I'd be ready to accompany Jacin to his meeting with the King.

"Yeah," he said, breathless too. "I know."

*Of course he does, you twat. He's in his twenties. He's not ten.*

He hopped over to the chair. With automatic movements, I brought the splint to him. Speaking of things that felt natural —being within arm's length of him didn't feel weird anymore. He didn't snap at me to back up, so some of his fear must have left too.

I was glad. And, strangely, the thought calmed my erection a little instead of the opposite. Still.

Pretending I'd left something in my room, I began to retreat.

"Icarus."

I whirled.

"Can you do the bottom of my foot?"

A laugh gusted out of me. My hands rose to my face and I scrubbed at my beard as I returned.

Of course. How could I have forgotten?

# 10

# JACIN

I was still half-hard as we prepared to leave. Maybe my king would like that. I doubted it, though.

The haze of arousal made me forget simple things, like the fact that Icarus didn't know the way to the King's chamber. I thought I remembered. If he walked behind me, I could lead him there.

I strapped on the splint, slowly securing the ties. The way Icarus had painted me was so different than Roshan. I felt bad comparing the two, but I couldn't help it. Roshan hadn't breathed against my lips or teased the end of my cock. He hadn't treated painting like adoration.

It felt so good I'd almost forgotten to step out of harm's way. Luckily, Icarus was careful, even though he felt dangerous. He hadn't touched me with anything but the brush, yet my skin tingled like it had after the Sun God ran his finger over my lips.

My own skin felt alien to me. It kept running over the moment Icarus painted my face with the care of sacred writing, or how he practically beat my balls with the end of the brush to turn them gold faster.

It was wrong to think like this.

Wrong, wrong, wrong.

And it kept my dick thick and heavy and painful for Icarus to see, clear as the lights in the King's chamber. He didn't mention it. He didn't have to.

Strangely resigned, I stood before the door to leave.

"You're not putting on any clothes?"

After what he'd just done, Icarus should have known better than to ask that question. "No. The King wants me this way."

Icarus stood to the side, offering to open the door. I gave him a little room, careful to reestablish some distance, and followed him out.

Natural, he had said. Of course it was natural to get aroused when a man with kind eyes, wearing a suit that showed off his shoulders, knelt right in front of you and painted your dick.

"Oh shit," breathed Icarus.

I turned.

"What do I call you again?"

I smiled. "My excellent ray, the Sun God's favorite."

A quick, temporary attraction didn't mean I was being disloyal to my king. The Sun God was still my favorite too.

"My excellent ray..." he repeated.

"That's it," I encouraged. The words fell like a familiar tune on my ears, but I already missed being called Jacin. If the King and I spent the night together, and if things were going well, maybe I could ask him to call me Jacin too.

"Make sure no one gets close to me," I added. "We'll go through this next room, I think, then right."

Icarus straightened his jacket. He looked nervous and brave and flustered. I bit my lip, then abruptly stopped to keep the paint in place.

When we emerged into the larger segment of the palace, Icarus's eyes grew huge, bouncing from the lavish design and high ceilings to the people who might walk too close to me. Though he stood shorter than I did, he had more muscle, and his focus on security didn't feel like Roshan's. I felt safe with Icarus.

By the time we reached the pillar and the glaring guard who'd destroyed my leg when it got in the way, my stomach was a coiled mass of nerves.

We halted. I nodded at Icarus.

"I am here escorting my excellent ray, the Sun God's favorite. He was summoned by the Sun God, King Lox, the high ruler of—"

"That's enough." The guard whipped out the gnarled stick again and held it out.

I didn't want to go through that crushing darkness again to travel like the deathless to the upper floor. But my king was waiting. Hopefully for a good reason. I couldn't shake off the apprehension that he'd discard me or worse.

I touched the staff.

A blinding, squeezing blackness wrapped around my ribs like a vise.

But it didn't last long. I was prepared for it this time. The fact made me absurdly proud of myself.

I took a few steps to the side to wait for Icarus to appear.

Gasping and spluttering, he careened to the floor the instant he appeared. His shoe touched the guard's boot.

Every muscle tensed so hard I felt I might crack in two. But Icarus was allowed to touch her. She wouldn't bash his face in for that. He just wasn't allowed to touch me.

My sight darkened and righted itself. Waves of panic flowed over me.

*Breathe*, came the memory of Icarus's voice.

I breathed.

By the time I opened my eyes again, he was standing. I shuddered with relief and took another step away from him.

I focused my attention on the King's cushioned platform, where he'd enjoyed time with other golden men to teach me how to please him. I'd failed terribly. Uneasily, I shifted my weight. My injured leg was healing by the day, and Icarus had added another feature—something about displacing weight?—to allow me to stand more easily.

The Sun King entered.

Icarus lowered himself until his face pressed to the floor.

I attempted a smile. This time, the glowing god wore a more contemporary white and gold outfit, not the flowing piece of fabric that came off so easily. He wore buckles and medals and two layers on top—a shirt and a jacket. He skirted around the steps to the bed he shared and approached me with purpose. I couldn't read his expression.

"Did you intend to touch your assistant?" the King barked.

I went cold. "Wha... What do you mean?"

"The one from before. Roshan." He said his name like it had an unpleasant taste.

A spear of dread pierced my chest. "No," I answered weakly. "Never."

His beautiful face relaxed a fraction, but he still had something on his mind. "Because you're only for me?"

"Only for you, my king." My heartbeat pummeled faster.

He gripped my chin in warm, strong fingers. My pulse hammered against his thumb as his gaze drifted over my face, down to my lips. He hummed, purring like a cat in the back of his throat.

Then he kissed me. I didn't have time to react. The jolt shot from where his lips crushed against mine down to my hands and toes. He tasted like oranges and leafy groves. Fingers pulled at my jaw, holding me against his mouth while he took what he wanted. Was I doing this right? Did he like that I opened my mouth so he could lick inside?

As sudden as the kiss had come, it stopped, leaving me dazed.

"That's good," he crooned.

I longed for more of his touch. A second kiss.

"Although," he continued, "I wouldn't have blamed you if it was intentional. Did you know Roshan well?"

"Not very well," I admitted, still tasting the King on my lips.

"We've discovered he was trying to infiltrate the palace, using you as the key to entry."

My head spun. "Really?" Roshan was closed off, but never seemed like a soldier or a spy. Maybe I just didn't know about things like that.

"And more are plotting every day." The King's hands closed

into fists before opening like flowers to gesture more freely. "They all want my power, my reign."

I opened my mouth to reply, but he kissed me again. I jumped, breathing hard around his angry lips. He was rougher than the first time, marking me as his own.

When he let go, I was hard again, but my lip was bleeding. I tasted its salt in my mouth. Confusion made me want to go back to my chamber. Maybe I could try it another day. Plots against the Sun God were so far out of my depth. And these kisses. They felt good, but... I couldn't have been doing it right.

"We can't have my rays threatened," he resumed, tucking a curl around my ear. "Laurel will go to your chamber later and explain what to do in a crisis." His eyes fell on Icarus, who hadn't raised his head. "And how to spot traitors."

# II

# ICARUS

On the walk back, Jacin's eyes had become dark and distant, a far cry from his usual buoyant spirits.

I understood why.

I'd had no idea the King was such an absolute fucker. I watched him with Jacin from the corner of my eye as I hunched with my forehead on the ground. He glowed—that part was real—but all he said about Jacin's last assistant, and the way he plucked kisses like he was pulling something out with his teeth that he wanted to spit out later.

I didn't know what to say. What was there to say? It sounded like Jacin's last assistant had been killed simply for brushing up against him.

No wonder he acted panicked if I got too close. Jacin was human, so his assistant didn't die of poisoned skin or something. It was murder. All because the King wanted to keep Jacin to himself.

I ground my teeth, watching Jacin's bare, golden feet walk on the white marble.

The bark-skinned woman had given me a key on the third day, so I pulled it out of my pocket when we reached what I thought was the right spot in the wall. That smooth expanse of expensive white stone had never looked more like a prison.

Choking on fury, I could barely fit the key in the lock. The worst part of all this—the King talking about threats to the palace, learning about the assistant's death, even the King's kisses—was the look on Jacin's face once we were alone. He looked so ashamed.

"I'm sorry I didn't tell you," he managed, scratching the back of his head and not meeting my eye.

I faced him, two paces away. "You didn't have to. You did everything you could to keep me safe."

He released a shaky breath.

I hated having to stay in this spot, but I couldn't move forward either. I couldn't hold him and reassure him that he deserved better than this.

"Will you be all right?" I asked. My hand floated up on its own and drifted back down.

He took a long time to answer, swallowing heavily a few times, blinking, brow furrowing as if making promises to himself. The movements on a shining golden face would have been absurd if it hadn't been him. It was like he'd retreated into himself with no memory that he was naked and painted. "Yes."

I didn't believe him.

"I didn't mean to touch him," he said quietly, desperately.

"I know you didn't."

"It was an accident."

The word jogged something new in my mind. An accident. "Is that how you got injured?" Shock and rage roared like a storm inside me. Deathless be damned. If the King hurt Jacin, I'd...

"I got in the way."

I took a half-step forward before I thought better of it. "No fucking way this is your fault."

His cheek crinkled in apologetic shame.

"It isn't," I said more firmly. "You would never hurt someone on purpose. If you got injured because"—I caught myself in time—"*someone* had a man killed, that isn't your fault. You should be able to touch whoever you want."

That last part wasn't supposed to come out.

But, fuck it, it was true. Even casually, as friends or in crowded rooms, a comforting hand on a shoulder, a hug.

More than a hug.

Jacin's eyes danced in the candlelight. "I'm the King's favorite. He doesn't want me to get hurt."

"Then how did that happen?" I snarled, gesturing to his leg.

"I shouldn't have touched him."

"Bullshit."

He lifted his chin. "Go to bed."

I stood a moment longer, nearly rushing forward to shake some sense into him. He deserved to be protected, and the Sun King was doing a shit job. From what I could see, I'd hate to know how he treated his least favorites.

"Yes, my excellent ray," I bit out. "Is that who you want to be?"

Stalking back to my little room, I heard Jacin speak one

more time, more composed now: "I know you're a good person, Icarus. I know you're not a traitor."

He didn't say the last thing he meant, but I heard it.

*So don't get yourself in trouble by acting like one.*

# 12

## ICARUS

I woke feeling like I had a hangover, even though I'd drunk nothing the night before. My argument with Jacin kept replaying in my mind.

I groaned as I sat up. If Jacin wanted to pretend that the King cared about him, he could. I was only his assistant, but the idea sent my hands into fists.

Dark shadows graced the corners of my small room. Sighing, I got out of bed. Breakfast would arrive soon. I'd ask if Jacin could try a portion of mine. If they said no, I'd scoop some of my food onto his plate anyway. Let their oppressive rules burn.

Out in the main room, Jacin sat in a steaming bath, holding a long-handled scrubber. Wet hair plastered against his forehead. He was still half-gold from his meeting with King Lox.

"Good morning," he said, more stiffly than usual.

Regret ghosted through me. "I... I'm sorry for yelling at you last night."

Jacin leaned forward in the water to reach his back. "I think I understand, but you can't do that anymore." He still wore a version of the dejected expression I'd seen last night. I wanted to wipe it off.

"Let me do that." I topped the steps and held out my hand for the scrubbing brush. Musk and lavender-scented steam rose against my skin. After the initial heady rush of aroma and the sight of Jacin's beautiful body, I wondered if these preparations were for the King again.

I didn't ask.

Jacin handed me the brush, the exchange careful but not afraid. A sliver of pride worked its way into me that he trusted me enough not to flinch when I got close. Now that I knew what had happened to his last assistant, it was no wonder he kept such a great distance for so long.

I dipped the brush in the hot water and scrubbed over Jacin's back and shoulders. He had handsome definition there, each muscle clear but not dry-tight, like some of mine could get after a week of labor with little more than tea. I'd put on some weight since arriving at the palace, and it made me feel more vital. I wished I had a metalsmith shop to visit. Jacin would probably enjoy seeing that too. He hadn't seen much in his twenty-four years.

"Have you always lived here at the palace?" I asked, the steam warming my face.

Jacin's head dipped down away from me. "No, but I was picked at a young age."

"Tell me about it." Hopefully I sounded soothing, the opposite of my demands from last night. I stood by my words, but Jacin deserved some comfort after what happened.

"I was the third son. We lived in Abru. My parents knew when I was a child that I was destined for the Sun God. They told everyone almost as long as I can remember. They were very proud of me. When I was eighteen, they presented me at the Pythigelia. He was there that year. I came straight to the palace and I've been here ever since." He kept his head bowed. Maybe it was easier to tell the story that way.

I hummed in acknowledgement. What parent would tell their child they'd be a god's consort? Jacin's good nature impressed me all the more. He had every reason for arrogance, yet he chose kindness every time. "Can I check if you have any more paint on you?" I asked softly.

"Yes, of course." He obediently turned, baring his gorgeous neck to me for the second time in two days. I scrubbed it clean. Water poured over his form in a way that left me in awe. His face, though serious, seemed to show he enjoyed the feeling of being washed. "My leg's doing better," he said.

One side of my mouth curled up. "Good."

"I can start exercising again. Please remind me."

"Okay." If I thought he was doing it for himself, I'd gladly exercise with him, but I suspected it was part of the expectation of belonging to the King.

Jacin sighed through parted lips. "That feels really good."

I kept the motion of the brush steady.

"I was afraid you'd hate me after what happened yesterday."

"I could never hate you," I whispered.

A knock at the door made me startle. I laughed at myself. When had I grown so jumpy?

"Breakfast," I said, setting down the brush where Jacin could reach it.

But it was more than just breakfast. I took the two plates from the server and backed up to let Laurel, the bark-skinned woman, into the room. Unlike most deathless beings, she didn't loom over me, but rose to my midsection.

"Emergency protocols," she said, clipped. She moved through the room as if she owned it. "Should we encounter an attack at the palace, you will move into this inner room." She indicated my door.

Jacin rose from the bath, snatching a towel not to cover himself, but to dry off his hair.

I missed Laurel's next words.

She seemed to be finished, because silence blanketed the room apart from the slight swish of water and the flicker of the candles.

"Are you expecting an attack?" I asked.

She frowned as though disrespected by my insolence. "Preparation is the weapon of the wise," she said.

Not an answer, though a fine proverb.

She went on. "We'll deliver the hooks today with the evening meal."

*Hooks?*

"Yes, my lady," I said. I'd gotten too comfortable speaking freely here. Not everyone was as accepting as Jacin, and, for many reasons, I needed to keep this job.

She pivoted to face Jacin. Not a trace of surprise crossed her face when she saw he was nude. "Most excellent ray."

And with that, she left.

As soon as the door shut behind her, I turned to Jacin. "Hooks?"

He looked confused. Frankly, it was adorable when he held his head to the side like that to scrub off his hair. "Did you not hear her?"

"Uh..."

"She said the hooks were to create a division down the room."

His words took a second to register. "Like with cloth or something?"

He smiled at my guess. "Yeah."

I set the two plates on the bed and sliced off a piece of my steak and potato pie with a fork, transferring it to Jacin's plate.

He seemed confused. "What are you...?"

"So you can taste it."

Jacin's meal consisted of his daily vial of healing potion, an egg, and three honey-covered strawberries. Now a chunk of pie leaked gravy unceremoniously toward the strawberries.

I left his plate on the bed and retreated a little way with mine. The food tasted delicious as always.

Jacin approached the food, limping on his bad leg, which didn't have the splint on. He cast me a nervous look. I gestured encouragingly with my fork. He sat beside the plate, the bed dipping with his weight, and stabbed a small piece of pastry crust wet with brown gravy.

"You won't be sorry," I said.

As if eating were a sin, he placed the bite between his lips carefully, judging the taste. After a second of chewing, his face split in a stomach-flipping grin. "That's so good!"

"Isn't it? Try the rest."

He did, making indecent noises I had no business hearing.

If a simple meat and potato pie could give him so much pleasure, I wanted him to try all my food. I wanted him to be safe and happy always.

I wanted to get him out of here.

# 13

## JACIN

I dreamed about the Sun God's kiss.

It wasn't a nice dream. I wanted more but my lips were poisoned. King Lox couldn't stop sucking on them, licking into my mouth. It felt good, but I wanted him to stop. Needed him to stop. I'd hurt him. But he pressed my head to his and took the poison into himself. I begged, trying to squirm away. Tears ran down my face. From the corner of my eye, I could see a body on the ground, a pool of blood growing from its head.

Then my vision was full of a bright glow, the King's glow, and he suctioned his mouth against mine. I couldn't breathe. I jerked and twisted, but he didn't move. He was already bigger than I was, and I hadn't been exercising, and he held the back of my head so I locked into place against him. I couldn't speak, had no air. My panicked whimpers had no effect. I fell—

Onto my bed.

I sucked in a loud gasp. I couldn't get enough air. My

bottom lids felt wet, so I roughly wiped them off with the back of my hand.

The dream had been so real. Had that really happened? I couldn't figure it out, and the uncertainty left me trembling.

The door on the other side of the room opened and Icarus stumbled out. In the dim light of a single lantern, his hair bent at crazy angles. He forced his arm through the sleeve of a shirt half-on. For a second, I saw his whole chest. It had lines of hair dark as the hair of his beard.

"Are you okay?" he asked in a rush. His voice was drowsy-deep.

It had to be the middle of the night. "I'm sorry," I said. "It's nothing."

He padded to the side of the bed anyway. I wished he would go back to sleep. My dream was starting to feel embarrassing. It hadn't happened.

It hadn't happened. I was all right.

"What's wrong?" he asked.

"Nothing."

"Can I get you something?"

"Just…" I sighed. "Water, please."

He nodded, reckless with sleep. A moment later, he returned with a cup. He set it on the table beside the bed next to a cold candle.

Once he backed away, I took it. The water calmed my racing thoughts a little.

He didn't return to his room but stood watching me. "If you asked for food or something, how would I get it? Should I walk out and find where it's prepared, or…?"

I didn't ask for much, since the King provided everything I

needed. I couldn't remember if I'd ever asked for extra food before. Maybe I should have, since Icarus's pie tasted so good. "I don't know, actually."

He hummed, a familiar sound now. "Where's the kitchen?"

"I don't know." I didn't think Roshan and I had passed it on the way to the King's chamber. Even if we did, I was too busy thinking about my meeting to notice. Hopefully Icarus wouldn't press.

A line furrowed across his brow. I hated feeling ignorant around him. I took another sip of water.

"You said that you arrived when you were eighteen, right?" he asked. "Did they take you through the door right out there, near this one?"

"I think so."

"No other entrance you remember?"

I squirmed and resettled. "No." This whole conversation made me anxious, although I couldn't have said why. Probably the dream wearing off. "Are you afraid of an attack?"

He shook his head, curls flopping. "I don't know if any of that's true. Even if there was an attack at the palace, I don't think anyone would come for us. They'd be targeting more important people."

"Right." The idea should have soothed me, but sourness rested in the pit of my stomach. I was the King's favorite. Wasn't that important?

Unless I wasn't his favorite anymore.

"Icarus?"

"Yes?"

I hesitated. "I know you didn't like the meeting with the King. I should have told you about Roshan." He opened his mouth, but I spoke over him. "My last assistant. That was his name. But..." I had no idea how to say this. Any way I phrased it in my mind left me blushing. Good thing it was dark.

I saw a thousand replies in Icarus's intense gaze, but he let the silence stretch.

It stretched so thin my breath shallowed. I took another drink and set the water to the side.

"I want the King to enjoy his time with me. I don't... know if he did last time." My whole face burned. I looked down at the covers. "Do you... have any suggestions?"

"Suggestions?"

I rushed on, haltingly. "You have seen more things than I have. I thought maybe... that you'd probably..." I ran out of air and stopped.

"What kind of suggestions?" Icarus asked slowly.

Maybe it had been a stupid thing to ask. Was this even appropriate for me to ask an assistant? I dismissed the thought. Roshan had been an assistant. Icarus was a friend. "Um, just, how to please him? I want him to love our time together. I want to be the best for him."

With all the uncertainty roiling in my gut and the shadow of nightmare all around me, I could do this one thing right—this most important thing.

If I couldn't please the King, he had every reason to choose a new favorite.

"I'm sure he's pleased with you now," Icarus said tightly.

Was my question annoying? Uncomfortable? I forced myself to go on. "I don't think I kissed him right."

Icarus's jaw hardened and flexed. He inhaled slowly. "A kiss should be enjoyed by both people." His tone was almost mechanical. "There isn't one right way to do it. Sometimes it's quick, just lips together. There's more... moving if there's passion involved."

He did know more. I knew it. "Can you explain it?"

"No." He took a step back, shaking his head like a spell had broken. "No, not tonight. The Sun King chose you for a reason. I'm sure he can teach you."

It felt better hearing sensitive information like this from a friend, though. The King was still a mystery to me in so many ways. I'd disappointed him before. If I could impress him next time, it might make all the difference.

But Icarus was already returning to his room.

"Do you need anything else?" he asked, not looking at me.

I wanted him to stay here while I slept. After the dream, having Icarus nearby grounded me. But that wasn't a kind or reasonable request.

"No. Good night! Thank you!"

He waved and I watched his back as it disappeared.

# 14

# ICARUS

When the Guardian appeared three days in a row, I got suspicious. Did they think I had touched Jacin? Did they think I was part of the rebel group his last assistant belonged to?

Whatever was causing all the extra checks and nervous servers was going to make it more difficult to help Jacin escape. The Sun King had obviously heightened his security.

I didn't know when my idea became an actual plan, but my first priority was getting Jacin out of this prison. If I had to leave my invention behind, so be it. No one I encountered seemed like the right person to show it to anyway.

Laurel, the bark-skinned woman, had her own business. The Guardian scanning Jacin for any transgression made me want to smash things, so she wasn't a good candidate either. I'd be damned before I presented it to the King.

Jacin hadn't brought up his question about pleasuring the King again, thank the gods. I thought I might poof into a pile of ashes. What sin had I committed that I was being tested like this? Everything he said and did made me want to draw him into my arms and show him what kisses were supposed to be like. And then our clothes would be gone and he'd cry out my name as he experienced more pleasure than the King could ever give him.

*Stop.*

But the voice had grown weaker. Caution wanted to step back when Jacin grinned at me or tried another new food. My crush had grown into an obsession I could do nothing about.

Unless I figured out a way to escape.

I said none of this to Jacin. He still wanted to be with the King, and the subject was too delicate to argue. If I started, I knew I'd end up cursing the one who could kill me and Jacin in a blink. Even though Jacin clearly didn't feel the same way about me, he deserved to be free.

I left our dirty supper dishes just outside the door for the servant. My mouth quirked at the crumbs left behind by the crusty, buttered loaf I'd been given. Jacin had eaten almost the entire thing.

"Get inside!"

My head jerked up. Two unfamiliar male guards were opening each door in the hall and yelling the same instructions before the doors slammed again.

"We're under attack. Get to safety!"

My heart jumped painfully as I shut the door fast.

"Jacin!" I yelled.

He stood from where he'd been doing push-ups. He met my eyes with concern.

"Get in my room."

"But—"

"Now!"

His sweaty chest rose and fell fast. "Get the curtains up."

"Get in the room," I bit out.

"Get the curtains up first."

"It's an emergency."

"You work for me!" he yelled.

I stopped in my tracks.

"Put up the curtains and then I'll go in." His eyes blazed with fear and determination.

I moved as fast as I could, hanging the godsdamned curtains along the ceiling to divide the room in two—one half for him and the other for me.

*If the King didn't have his fucking rule...*

There were two curtains so they could flow in both directions, preventing the possibility of accidentally touching underneath if one of them moved. The curtains fell in the exact center of my little bed and I didn't take the time to move it, so there wasn't room for either of us on there.

My head and mouth were full of curses by the time I finished.

"Come on!" I shouted.

I didn't think attackers would come for Jacin, but that didn't mean it was impossible. His assistant had been killed, after all.

"Get in here, damn it! I'm against the far wall."

My side of the room included the door, so I saw him enter. He was visibly shaking and hurried to his side of the curtain.

"You okay?" I asked. I'd yelled at him again. I doubted that helped his anxiety about an already stressful situation.

"Do the curtains move?"

"No, they won't move. You have your side over there."

"There's no way…?"

I tried to calm down. "No. They're thin, but they won't come down off the hooks and there's no way to reach underneath unless you intentionally crawl under there. You're safe." I moved toward the door. "It'll be dark when I shut the door," I warned.

"That's okay." He still sounded too breathless.

I eased the door closed with us inside. "I don't know how long we have to be in here," I confessed.

The sound of labored breathing flowed from the other side of the curtain.

"Deep breaths," I said. "No one is going to come in here. No one will hurt you. If they try, I'll stab their eyes out."

"What if there's a hole in the curtain?"

I finally understood the reason for Jacin's panic. It wasn't the attack. It was about being trapped in a small room with me.

I moved to the foot of the divided bed where I assumed Jacin stood on the opposite side. "You won't touch me. Nothing can happen."

A thick sniff.

I mentally cursed King Lox and the fucking gall it took to kill Jacin's assistant in front of him, and harm Jacin in the process.

*Good luck, rebels.*

"It's okay," I said. "Let's just… try to sleep. Who knows how long we'll have to stay, and it's nighttime already." I felt like I was rambling. Hopefully some of this was helpful. "We'll just rest."

On the other side of the curtain, Jacin blew out a breath. "I'm sorry."

"Don't apologize."

"It's not you."

"I know."

We stood for a few moments in silence.

"I'm going to lie down on the floor at the foot of the bed," I explained, lowering myself. "There's not enough room up there."

"Okay." The curtains rustled next to me. Jacin was doing the same thing.

My heartbeat picked up again. We hadn't stood this close since I painted him. If the curtains weren't there...

I rolled up my thickest jacket and placed it under my head for a pillow. "Will you be all right sleeping on the floor?"

"I'll be fine." It sounded like his breathing was back to normal. Good. The fabric couldn't block the smell of sweat and oranges coming off him. It left me lightheaded.

When he spoke again, the whisper came right next to my ear, so close his voice sounded a little deeper than usual. "I'm sorry. I don't... It has nothing to do with you. I'm glad you're here."

"I'm glad I'm here too."

"You're the best friend I've had in a long time, and I'm... I don't know."

My entire abdomen felt like a coil of snakes. Blood roared in my ears. I watched him shift in the slack from the curtains.

"I wish I didn't have to be this careful," he said. "It's not your fault."

"If we were different people, we wouldn't have to be this careful."

Then the world shifted sideways.

My heart leapt to my throat.

The curtain pushed outward, just a little, and the outline of Jacin's finger rested against mine. Several furious heartbeats later, he pushed further, covering three of my fingers in a gentle squeeze before retreating.

I lay blinking at the dark ceiling. *Don't overreact.* But my body and mind were rushing so fast I could hardly breathe.

"What would you do, if we were different people?" Jacin asked.

My skin buzzed with danger. So much danger.

But he sounded sincere. Was I just reading vulnerability in the question where there was none?

"What would you want me to do?" I squeaked before clearing my throat.

"It would be nice for you to put a hand on my shoulder."

"I can do that."

"What else?" Jacin's voice was quiet but clear.

"If we were different people, maybe I'd give you a hug." *Still a friendly thing to do. Not like I'd want to ride him.*

"I'd hug you back."

*Oh fuck.* "...More?" I asked.

"Mm hm."

My cock was definitely getting in on the conversation now. "Maybe I give you a kiss on the cheek." I said it lighter than I'd said anything so far. That way, Jacin could retreat if he wanted to. No harm done.

"I like that."

I could hardly swallow around my pulse. "If we were different people, would you want more?"

"I bet a different version of me would want to try it."

"Okay." My hands were clammy. "I give you soft kisses along your jaw. Is that good?"

"Very good." It was hard to read his tone, but he seemed totally focused, at least. His panic was gone.

"All the way to your chin. Should I kiss your mouth?"

This wasn't real. This couldn't be happening.

"Yes."

*Oh gods, oh gods...* Did he really want this? If I went any further, he'd hear how obsessed I was with him. But he insisted on playing pretend. If I went too far, I could claim I was pretending along to distract him from his fears.

"Then," I said, "I kiss your mouth, slowly at first. Softly. My arms are around you, holding you."

Jacin sighed. "What else?"

"More?"

"More."

I'd grown so hard it was difficult to focus on forming coherent sentences. "I kiss you harder... and... start rocking against you."

The rhythm of Jacin's breathing quickened.

I kept going, delirious. "I run my hand down your chest, then your stomach..." I followed the motions on my own body as I spoke. "And then I reach carefully down the front of your pants."

A new rhythmic sound told me he already reached the next part. He made a small, straining noise that traveled straight to my balls.

"I wrap my fingers around you. Are my fingers there?"

"Mm hm." There was a whimper in the response.

*I might die here.*

"I start stroking you up and down, running my thumb around the head. When you're... hard, I pump faster." I could barely get the words out, my hand worked so furiously.

Fuck, I wouldn't last.

*Fuck!*

"Can I..." he panted, "touch you too?"

"Gods, yes." I groaned loudly, too turned on to care anymore.

When Jacin grunted hard, I lost control, exploding my cum with more gasping force than I'd ever experienced in my life.

# 15

# JACIN

I woke from a deep sleep, sticky with my own cum. Where was I? The room was dark. My back ached from lying on the floor without moving for so long. I leaned against something hard and warm through hanging sheets.

In a heady torrent, the night came back to me.

Icarus telling me exactly how he'd touch me if he could. My body aflame as he kept talking. He *had* to keep talking. His words were like the hands that weren't allowed to touch my skin.

The way he was so careful with me, checking how far I wanted to go. With each step, I wanted to go further.

It was like I'd never really heard his voice before, so rough and gentle. It tasted better than meat and potato pie.

As soon as I imagined his touch, the idea struck me like a shock of heat. I hadn't realized how cold I was. I wanted Icarus to talk and touch and *be* with me in every way he could. Until I was gripping myself, making wet noises he must have heard. Those desperate sounds that ripped from his throat…

I was lengthening, hard as a rod again.

The object against my back and biceps moved. I gasped.

The curtains? They hadn't shifted?

Icarus's warm voice checked in on the other side of the barrier. "Everything all right?"

A pang of embarrassment coursed through me. He was actually there, the real Icarus, and I'd tugged myself dry right next to him.

I reached blindly around for something to wipe off my bare chest. I'd hate for him to see me like this. Our conversation felt like a fever dream. How was I supposed to face him now? What if it wasn't real?

"Yes," I said. "Good morning. I just... didn't realize I'd be here." Tentatively, I settled back down, pressed up against him through the cloth. His solid heat felt so good I wanted to stay next to him for another night's sleep, where things weren't real and last night wouldn't matter.

If we were different people, I might love him instead.

I drew up the draping end of the curtain and rubbed the cum off myself. This was a disaster.

"Do you like being here?" he asked.

*Yes, yes, yes.* "What do you mean?"

His shoulder jostled against mine so lightly I might have imagined it. Every twitch he made left my head spinning. I had probably broken so many rules. I couldn't tell the King.

"Here," said Icarus.

My heart slammed fast against my ribs.

*Yes. I want to stay here.* This sensation was so new and exhilarating it hurt.

"Did you mean it?" I whispered.

His body tensed. Just a tiny movement, but I craved every one. "I don't want to make your life harder, Jacin," he said carefully.

*Say my name again. I've never liked it more than when it's in your mouth.* Icarus made me feel reckless and safe and powerful, and, right now, afraid.

Because he didn't say no.

"I loved it," I blurted. Flames raced up my cheeks.

A breathy chuckle of relief gusted from Icarus. "Good. I didn't want you to avoid me because I defiled you or something. I want, all the time, to be like this, to be close to you. I..."

My heart charged on, hard and painful.

"I've never met someone like you," he continued as if pushing words through a barrier. I held my breath to listen. "I can't get enough. I know you belong to someone else, but I want you like I want my own body. And... fuck, I want to touch you so much I feel like my skin will burn off if I have to see you naked one more time." A smothered groan told me he probably held his face in his hands. "I'm sorry."

"Don't apologize," I wheezed. He told me that all the time. "I didn't know I was... bothering you so much."

"Not bothering! Most people go a lifetime without seeing anything as perfect as your body."

Fiercely pleased, I grimaced to myself. Pleasure and agony crashed against each other like waves. I wanted to match his... declaration of love. That was what it sounded like. And I did love him—at least, I never wanted him from my side and, after last night, his name had become intertwined with urges I didn't know I had.

But I couldn't say that. I was still the Sun God's favorite, for now.

Maybe afterward, when I aged, and I wasn't fit to be his consort, he'd let me go and I could retire into Icarus's arms.

"I want something like that again. With you," I said. I sighed. "I wish we could actually touch." My hand inched down at the mere mention, teasing my sensitive length.

"We can be whatever you need," he replied, eager. I heard a hint of disappointment there too.

"I need... you," I whispered into the sheet. My reward was a shiver in the arm pressed next to mine.

# 16

# ICARUS

"My excellent ray!" called an unfamiliar voice, muted through the door. No panic or urgency bled through. The attack—if one had existed at all—was probably over.

I grumbled but forced myself to stand. Sensing Jacin's firm arm next to mine for hours as we rested was paradise. Now, this stranger had ruined it.

Bleary, I lurched toward where the door was in the dark. I hadn't gotten any sleep. Between the shape of Jacin next to me and my mind relentlessly mocking me with my own words over and over (*"I don't want to make your life harder"—well, you fucked that one up, didn't you?*), I was a mess.

Literally too. Hopefully I didn't get cum on the curtain. Probably did, though.

After I opened the door, I called back to Jacin, "You can come out. I'm far enough away." I gave a bitter chuckle. I felt like I'd all but given him a blowjob, but we still couldn't stand closer than arm's length. He belonged to the god, not to me.

*So stupid.* But my heart wouldn't listen. It yearned for him so deeply I doubted I could ever overcome the ache.

Stepping farther away from my door, I checked myself quickly to make sure there was no visible evidence on my clothes of what we'd done. Fine. It was fine.

Jacin emerged after me. His face softened uncertainly when he saw me. Gods, that messy tiredness was sinful.

But we had no time for awkwardness, because his gaze shifted away from mine and he stiffened. In a second, he turned on a smile, still somehow genuine and welcoming. "Good morning," he greeted.

The Guardian approached. I took another step back, body heating. Jacin and I hadn't touched, but would her mystical deathless power be able to tell what we'd done?

"The danger is past," she said from beneath her cloak. "Approach."

Jacin's leg still didn't match the rest of his golden skin, but he could hobble without the splint now. The green vial he took every day would have been helpful in the Labyrinth.

The Guardian stood close to him.

My hand itched to make her back up. Could she smell the truth on us? I did my best to look nonchalant.

Her glowing eyes scanned him from his hair to his feet.

"You have remained loyal to our king, the Sun God."

I had no outward reaction, though relief flooded my veins. Jacin gave a close-lipped smile to the Guardian.

We'd gotten away with it. I hadn't broken either of us by saying I craved him. Pretending his fingers pumped my cock didn't tip off the King's emissary. My head felt like a cloud. I could have jumped off a cliff, trusting I'd fly instead of falling.

The Guardian left as she always did, stoically, quickly, as if she had other people to visit.

As soon as the door closed, I locked eyes with Jacin. Neither of us spoke for a minute. His deep-set gaze filled with questions.

Did he regret it now?

"Breakfast will be here soon."

Of all the things he could have said, I couldn't say I expected that one.

"What?"

"Breakfast." He didn't step toward me, but he looked beautifully flushed.

"Why does breakfast matter?" It was, once again, a stupid thing to say.

He thought for a moment before answering. "We still can't touch, but... breakfast is the last visitor until supper." Hope lit his eyes. "Maybe... you could teach me things. Or we could just spend time together?" He bit his lip.

I wanted to tease him and say we spent all our time together already, just to get him to gnaw that perfect lip more. But I nodded instead. "I'd like that. I'll always like that."

An idea formed. When I grinned, so did he.

WE'D NEVER EATEN BREAKFAST SO FAST.

I hadn't had the chance to invent something new since the splint, which Jacin used less and less. Despite the voice in my head that kept trying to get me to think rationally, Jacin—his whisper about needing me, the cautious optimism in his smile, the raging attraction I experienced every time I stood in the same room—drew me back like a tidal wave.

Today, I didn't care that he belonged to the King. The King could go hang. Today, I had Jacin to myself, and the freedom to invent ways to please him, as long as we didn't brush skin to skin.

"What are you doing?" he asked as I dragged a wooden chair over to the bed.

"Setting up a curtain," I said.

He huffed, but his eyes sparkled as he watched me.

"It's so we don't get too close. I want to try something."

He sat on the edge of the bed a couple paces away from the chair. I had trouble focusing when he looked at me like that. Until last night, he hadn't acted interested in me. A block of wood would have been interested in Jacin. Having his attention like this, knowing he enjoyed when I turned him on, was headier than wine (which he'd never tried.)

He watched as I pulled the side table with candles over to the chair. I could practically see his mind working.

"Do you know what I'm going to do?" I asked, teasing.

"No."

A hint of awkwardness stretched between us since our time on opposite sides of the curtain, but it was a fragile, almost tender thing. I didn't want to push him too hard.

"Then do you trust me?"

His response was totally open. "Yes." No caveat. No conditions.

I was so in love with him it hurt.

I tried to swallow on a dry mouth. "I'm going to stand on this chair with the back to you so it will block the space between us." I patted the chair as if I were selling it. "I won't touch you."

"I know."

My pulse throbbed in my throat and my dick. "Would you lie down? Here?" I gestured to the part of the bed closest to me.

He scooched over while I stepped back, giving him room to feel comfortable. He lay down with his legs hanging off the end of the bed. "Like this?"

He'd obey most orders even if he didn't want to. It hardly mattered that I was his assistant. The role was invented to keep him pristine and appealing to the King. His whole life had been for someone else, never himself.

I paused.

"Am I not doing it right?" he asked.

"You're perfect." I revised. "You're doing it the right way."

He turned his head to look at me. Waiting for more instructions.

"If any of this makes you uncomfortable," I said, "just tell me. We'll stop. You can say no to anything I suggest and I won't be angry."

His lips quirked. If I could have devoured them, I would have. "Okay. I don't think I'll want to stop."

Did he have any inkling how much he turned me on? "But if you change your mind, tell me."

"I will."

I exhaled. "I'm going to stand on this chair and lean over you." The next part was weird. And maybe painful. But inventive solutions sometimes started that way and ended up making breakthroughs. If I were the one lying on the bed, I'd want Jacin to do this to me. Hopefully he felt the same. "And," I said, "I'd like to pour hot wax on your body."

His crotch bulged, and his pupils blew so large his eyes went black. "Is this... something I'll need to know?"

The reminder of his other so-called lover doused my hard-on in cold. "No," I confessed, the word clipped enough that he probably heard the bitterness behind it. "This is just for us. If you still want it."

He nodded, his loose curls splaying against the deep red blankets. "That sounds good." His voice was breathless. A flush grew down his bare chest. "Do you want my clothes on?"

My mind blanked.

Completely blanked.

"I can keep these on." Jacin looked at me curiously, thumb hooking in his waistband.

There wasn't enough air. When would he get it through his head that his nudity *did* something to me? To him, it was obviously normal.

"Off."

I hadn't given my mouth permission to say it. *Fuck. I'm an idiot.*

But I watched him as if he held the secrets of the universe while he stripped off his pants and left them on the floor. His cock bounced up against his flat lower stomach. He didn't acknowledge it.

When he lay back down, stretched out like that, *for me*, I doubted I could climb the chair at all. Curse words tumbled uselessly through my head. None of them were right.

I forced myself to focus on the candle on the end table. I dipped the tip of my finger in the red wax to test the temperature. Warm, but not scalding. I didn't want to leave any marks on Jacin's perfect skin.

"Ready?" I asked when I could speak.

"Yes. I'm excited."

Holding the candle, I mounted the chair on my knees instead of standing up. Seemed safer. Jacin smiled encouragingly at me, tensing for the new sensation.

"Pretend the wax is me touching you," I said under my breath. I plucked the candle from its tall stand and tilted it to judge the wax's tipping point.

I was glad the wooden back of the chair hid how stiff I was. Considering what we were doing, it shouldn't matter, but still.

I began in the center of his chest, letting a bead of red wax spill to judge the temperature. He flinched when it dropped, his body eager.

"Too hot?"

"No. Keep going."

This time I drew a line from that center drop to his right pectoral, so perfectly toned. When I soaked his nipple in wax, he gasped and arched. I needed that sound again.

The candle had to burn down a little between bloody-looking lines, but Jacin waited patiently. The next line drenched his other nipple.

"Oh, yes," he breathed.

"You like that?"

"Yes."

I felt wild. A second candle was lit too. Why not use that? I reached down and didn't bother taking it out of its holder.

Lines of wax pooled in the delectable space down the middle of his abs.

I'd seen his cock dozens of times, but didn't realize how long it got when he was hard. He whimpered, twitching at each new drop.

I veered off toward his hip, drawing on part of his lower stomach not covered by his erection.

"That's not…" he murmured.

I tipped both candles back up.

He opened his eyes. "I'm not in shape anymore, so that part is too soft. You don't have to do that part."

My mouth fell open. If he'd allowed it, I would have kissed every morsel of his "too soft" parts. His stomach right below his navel barely filled out at all, merely softening the cut lines into something more real. "That's a load of bullshit." Recklessly, I poured a thin stream of wax over the tip of his cock. He bucked and squeezed his eyes closed. "You have the body of a god. Anyone who makes you feel unworthy can get eaten by sea monsters." I worked the wax down his shaft. With all his writhing, I didn't even know if he could understand what I was saying. "You are desirable, and beautiful, and good. You are more than any piece of your body. I'd still want to be beside you, doing this…"

Suddenly, Jacin sat up.

I reared back, almost falling off the chair. Ungracefully, I stepped off backward, managing not to drop the candles. Jacin's hand, covered in thick, dripping wax, worked fast. He was moaning, delirious, and in seconds he came hard, ruining the picture I'd painted on his skin.

## ❧ 17 ❧

## JACIN

I panted in the aftermath, only aware afterward that maybe I wasn't supposed to finish myself off. After last night, it didn't feel taboo. But Icarus had made such incredible plans to please me, maybe he wanted them to go a certain way. He seemed to enjoy bending over me, dripping wax in designs only he could see. Inventing erotic games we shouldn't play because we both wanted to play them.

"I..." I stopped myself from apologizing. "Maybe I shouldn't have done that."

I met Icarus's gaze. His lightly bearded mouth had gone slack, eyes glazed with lust. "I told you, you can do what you like," he croaked.

"I liked that." It came out as a groan.

Wax dripped down the sides of the tall candles in his hands. They looked... phallic.

When had I started thinking this way?

Icarus set down the candles and fetched a towel for me to clean off. The candle wax had partially cooled and hardened.

My hands were covered with shards of pliant red. Peeling the soft coins of wax off my nipples made me wince with pleasure again.

"It's not fair for just me—" I began.

"It's fine."

Looking down at the cloth covered in wax, concern budded in my chest. Wouldn't someone see this? Would they wonder why wax had spilled everywhere?

"Let's not do that again."

Icarus frowned. "I thought you liked it."

*Like* didn't describe it. It wasn't only the delicious sensation of heat teasing my sensitive parts, it was Icarus's words. They seduced me more than the wax. Icarus had lower standards than the King. With Icarus, I wouldn't have to be scented like orange blossoms with a physique created from strenuous exercise and pomegranate seeds and oysters. I could simply be Jacin.

"I did, but no one can know," I said.

"No one's coming until supper."

Dread grew into a knot in my chest. I stood and pulled my pants back on over my newly growing cock. Hopefully it would settle down.

"You shouldn't have to live like this," he said, moving to stand in front of me. He approached as close as the Guardian did for her checks. He smelled like sweat and arousal and something forest-sweet. His brown eyes had a ring of gold in them, like the sun.

My heartbeat fluttered wildly in my throat. "Get back."

Hurt crossed Icarus's eyes, but he obeyed.

This had been a mistake.

"If you weren't here anymore, we wouldn't have to worry about accidentally touching," he said.

"I know." I sounded too surly. It was wrong to be ungrateful, with all that I'd been given—life at the palace, my every need cared for, the favor of the King, and the best person I knew to serve as my assistant.

"So," he said, voice tantalizingly low, "why can't we leave?"

"We can't leave," I said automatically. At best, Icarus would face Roshan's fate, and I couldn't live with myself if that happened.

"I bet I could figure out a way. You deserve better than this." Icarus's eyes burned.

I raised both eyebrows. "Better than *this*? This is the royal palace of Hyperion. I'm chosen by the Sun God. There is nothing better than this. Everything I have is a gift."

"You're kept in a cage, Jacin—"

"I can't jeopardize this. I can't jeopardize *you*. I... I made a mistake."

Icarus stepped forward again. I scrambled backward onto the bed. The chair, pressed against the mattress, tipped forward and back with the motion.

"I wasn't going to touch you," he said, pain and anger radiating from his eyes.

"You said you wouldn't be angry. This is what I need right now. If we keep playing, one day we'll make a mistake. No."

Icarus gripped his hands together as if to ground himself. "Haven't I been careful with you?"

This was awful. "Yes! Obviously, you have. You've been wonderful. And, I was thinking, we could just wait."

He searched my face as if it held the answer of what I meant.

"Until I'm older," I finished.

"You're twenty-four now." His scarred hands broke apart and one squeezed up the length of his forearm. He hardly seemed aware of what he was doing. "You're an adult."

"Yes," I said with a humorless laugh. "I mean older like forty."

Icarus's eyes widened with understanding. His jawline hardened. "When the King doesn't want you anymore. When he throws you out like you're worthless to him."

"He has high standards for his consorts, especially his favorite. He's allowed to. He's the Sun God."

"Fuck him!" Icarus spat.

"Icarus!"

"No, fuck him!" His flexed arms trembled. "Fuck him for making you feel like you aren't good enough, keeping you in this room like a little pet. Fuck him! He doesn't even visit you. Jacin, you're not his favorite."

My breath stalled. "I am."

"No, you're not. They call you the sixteenth ray—"

"That doesn't mean anything."

"—so I think the King gets off on fucking dozens of beautiful people like they're things to use. He has a harem of sixteen, twenty?"

My face burned. The memory of watching him having sex with all those people at once brought bile to the back of my throat. It wasn't possible. He wanted me to learn, because I was the favorite. "No."

"You know he does. You're worth *more* than being the sixteenth hole for him to—"

"Stop!" I stood on the bed, looking down on Icarus, who was already shorter than me. "Stop! You're wrong. He's given me everything I have. I am *proud* to be his."

Icarus's face contorted, but he didn't snap back a retort. Dark brows lowered over his piercing eyes.

I was so greedy. I wanted him to love me too. I thought I might be sick.

*Would you wait for me?*

I didn't ask the question aloud. It was overtly selfish. I saw that now. But my whole body blazed to hear the answer.

My mouth opened, closed. A plea echoed through my being. Maybe Icarus saw it. I couldn't do any better than this. If he could wait, then I'd have done my service to the King and we could finally indulge the impulses he stirred so deeply in me. He was my best friend, and every time I thought about him, I wanted him close to me. Closer even than that. Touching. Rubbing that great, terrible ache I felt all over.

Finally, Icarus puffed a bitter laugh through his nose. It felt like he was falling or I was falling and we couldn't catch each other. "I understand. No more games. That's all you had to say."

# ICARUS

I couldn't even blame Jacin. He'd grown up his entire life being fed that drivel about what an honor it was to be chosen by the King. Of course he'd choose King Lox, the Sun God, over me.

The very idea I could compete was idiotic.

That didn't mean my heart didn't break, though.

For a minute, I had thought maybe we could work. Jacin said he needed me, whispered it into my ear after I'd confessed I couldn't breathe without him.

The problem with waiting until the King finished using him was that I couldn't protect him from that feeling of inadequacy. Years would go by before I could hold him and try to repair all the damage King Lox had done. Even if Jacin never chose me at all, I wanted him safe.

The next couple days were quieter than usual. No new attacks, just new gossip from the kitchen staff. Daily visits from the Guardian. Jacin looking guilty while I could do nothing.

With every task, I tried not to show how upset I was. Every movement of the scrubber or word I spoke after that, I attempted both the distance Jacin wanted and unrelenting care. If he wanted the King, that was his choice.

But I could show him what it was like to be loved.

He showed me. Even at odds, he never failed to say good morning and offer a smile to start the day. Whenever he spoke, he told the truth. At least, the truth as he knew it. He never tried to hurt me. No matter how many times I reminded myself, it only hurt more to know that someone so open and kind would be trapped here.

Jacin used bars I hadn't noticed my first week to pull himself up. He worked out all the time now.

The breakfast plates I hadn't set in the hall yet showed his food on one and mine on another. No crossover.

He huffed out rhythmic breaths, pulling himself up again and again. His sweat-stained torso and veined arms didn't need any more exertion today, unless it was to torture me.

I readjusted myself and continued cleaning the bath, currently drained of water. My sleeves were rolled up to the elbow and I'd taken off my shoes. A sheen of water remained in the bottom, wetting my feet.

He was almost out of orange blossom oil. I'd ask for more at the next meal, since neither of us were getting out of here. I dipped my fingers against the top of the bottle and tipped out oil. Drawing an arc around the lip of the tub, I smeared the oil on the edge so Jacin could smell it better when he bathed.

A knock.

Probably the Guardian again.

I climbed out of the tub, but Jacin, on the far end of the room, kept doing exercises. Yes, I was right. The Guardian.

She swept by me, a tall shadowy ghost keeping Jacin in line. He stepped forward. Again, she declared him pure enough for the King. I unclenched my hands.

Because she was deathless and Jacin respected her, I couldn't punch her in those judgmental glowing eyes of hers. Who was she to say that Jacin was enough or not?

"The King requires you in an hour."

My chest stopped moving.

"An hour?" Jacin repeated.

The Guardian turned to me for the first time since I'd met her. "Paint quickly."

I set scented oils in an array near Jacin's feet. There was no time to bathe.

"Thank you," he said, sweaty and more disheveled than I'd seen him since... well, since I made him come. Twice. "What if—?"

"He'll be very pleased with you."

"I have gotten stronger," he said, looking down.

The only difference I noticed was his skin sticking more closely to his muscles.

Nervous energy kept me moving. *Don't stop, then you can't think.* "Yes," I said. "Choose a scent and then I'll paint you."

He chose orange blossom, as I expected he would, patting it all over the top half of his body.

I fetched the gold paint and long brush. He got naked again. I swore he spent half his time that way.

I felt like I was outside myself, watching. Not involved.

Something about how he planted his feet to curl slightly and look down was so beautiful. The lines of his body sharp and un-self-conscious. He had a range of beauty I doubted Queen Cytherea herself could match.

I painted. His light bronze skin became gold under the brush. I did my job, painting for King Lox. When thoughts grounded me into the moment again, I imbued my strokes with care. The rest of the time, he was a piece of parchment I needed to color in. He wasn't muscles and lips and deep eyes.

Attempting to paint his cock in an un-erotic way was especially challenging. My eyes glazed over with hopelessness. He'd know I tried.

The lines weren't as precise as last time, but I got him completely covered. He glistened again, a gorgeous object.

He didn't remind me once not to get too close.

I forced air back in my lungs once I finished, tossing the brush into the pot of gold paint. "You're all ready."

"I think this is it," he said, eyes big with worry and anticipation.

I blinked rapidly a couple times. "He'll be so pleased with you. You've been... working hard for him. The Sun God." My attempt to give his title as cajoling encouragement didn't work out as planned.

"Yes," Jacin breathed. "I hope he wants me this time." He

met my eyes. They softened at the corners. "And that doesn't mean—"

"It doesn't matter," I said quickly. "I hope you... enjoy... whatever happens."

My heart had shriveled to a blackened crisp.

"Thank you." His cheek dimpled.

"Let's go."

I led the way this time. The palace wasn't confusing like the paths of the Labyrinth, plus I didn't want to follow Jacin's perfect ass. All my pining was creepy enough at this point without adding that.

We reached the pillar quickly. The tall, gruff guard was there.

"The King called for my excellent ray, the Sun God's favorite," I said.

She drew the short, gnarled staff from her belt and held it out. We traveled through crushing darkness to the King's chamber. That mode of travel got easier. Was it the staff that let us travel like that, or was it the deathless guard's power extending to the staff? Father would love to have one of those to travel to the university, if he could get used to it.

Better to think about that. Better to think about *anything* besides what would happen to Jacin in the next hour.

I watched the guard pocket the staff on her hip next to a brutal-looking bludgeon with metal accents. I peered more closely. Was that pattern...?

"Here he is. Come up with me!"

I jerked my gaze away to see King Lox emerge into the room. He held his arms wide. Even though the god literally glowed, I couldn't stop looking at Jacin, who cast me an excited look before approaching the raised part of the room where the King waited.

"Leave us," the King commanded.

Numbly, I watched as Jacin climbed the shallow steps. His back looked stiff. He was nervous.

Something prodded my hand. The gnarled staff.

I gripped it and materialized downstairs at the base of the pillar. The guard sheathed the staff again. I could have sworn I'd seen that other weapon before, the one of wood and leather and metal. That pattern looked so familiar.

It was her. The guard. She had hurt Jacin and killed that other assistant.

Heat filled me so violently I thought I might explode.

"Return to your room. We'll call you when the ray is finished to pick him up," she said. No concern showed on her grim face.

What else could I do?

*Plot how you can kill her and not get Jacin in trouble—that's what you can do.*

Vibrating, I picked up each foot as if they were weights and slowly made my way back to our room.

I was doing the right thing, wasn't I? It didn't feel like it, when all I could picture was either stabbing that smug guard in the neck or the King bending Jacin over.

By the time I arrived, I felt genuinely sick. I had to find a place to throw up. Maybe a nap after that.

*Should I rush back there?*

*No. Jacin made up his mind. And the guard who hurt him is deathless. You wouldn't have a chance against her.*

*That shouldn't matter. Not when it's to avenge someone else.*

*No, no, no...*

I put the key in the lock, but the door swung open at the pressure before I turned it. Had I left the door unlocked? I didn't think so.

Poking my head in, I pushed aside the curtains. Voices rose around the space.

Two guards stood in an overturned mess of the chamber— the same two male guards who had warned about an attack and sent us to safety in my room. The covers on Jacin's bed were twisted, pillows littered the floor, a few of the larger bottles had been overturned on the ground, creating viscous puddles...

"What are you doing?" I roared, charging forward. "What the fuck is this?"

"We're looking for evidence of insurrection," one of them replied calmly.

The other held up an object I knew very well. I'd spent months perfecting it, obsessing over every detail in the forge. "And I think we found it."

## ❧ 19 ❧

## JACIN

For the first time in my life, I was alone with the King. My heart ran so fast I struggled to keep up.

His ethereal beauty drew me in as if he were the sun, glowing on the horizon. I'd waited so long for this. My whole life.

As my foot hit the first soft cushion at the top of the dais, I studied him, trying to memorize everything. The coins and statues and paintings didn't capture what it was like to be in King Lox's presence. I'd known *about* him for as long as I could remember, but I wanted to know *him*.

"Come here," the King urged again, pulling me by the arm to join him in the center under the cluster of lights. My forearm tingled where he'd touched it.

"Yes, my king," I said. My voice didn't sound like my own.

A graceful woman I'd never seen before appeared and began opening doors along the rim of the small room. More gold-painted people were—

My thoughts smothered under the King's mouth on mine.

He gripped my hand and placed it between his legs. He wore a draped piece of clothing, but I could feel the hard line of his cock under my palm. He ground into it.

We weren't going to talk for a minute first?

The pillow I was standing on depressed as more people joined us on the platform. I wasn't alone after all.

I was almost glad.

The King hadn't said anything or asked or even run his hand over my jaw like he did before. I yelped as he grabbed my penis and pulled. Was that what he wanted me to do to him? I tried copying the movement. He growled into my mouth.

Okay, I could do that.

He broke off our kiss to allow one of the other consorts to remove his clothing. As soon as the fabric was pulled out from between us, he grabbed me again hard enough that his fingernails scratched. He pushed my head down wordlessly toward his groin, the expectation sunbeam-clear.

Panic welled up like blood. I was supposed to do this, but I didn't want to. Icarus would say I didn't have to. The King hadn't even looked at me after first inviting me up with him.

He gripped and held himself out.

I didn't even really know him. Did he care what positions I wanted to try or what ideas I had? And why so many people? I was looking into two mirrors facing each other, so my face reflected over and over and over and…

"I feel sick," I muttered.

The King's hand clawed my hair and pressed down so I faced his hard cock. He was big. I could choke.

The cooing voices of the others rang through the air above.

"Touch me, my king."

"I need your cock inside me."

"Choose me."

"I feel sick," I said, louder. "I want to make this good for you, so can I come ba...?"

Glowing hips shoved forward. Uncertainly, I opened my lips.

Icarus would never make me do this. I didn't feel lost in the King the way I felt lost in Icarus when he merely spoke to me.

The salty end of the King's cock forced into my mouth. Holding the back of my head against his groin, he gave a thrust so sharp I gagged. I couldn't breathe. His massive length blocked my throat, sliding all the way down.

I didn't want this. At all. I wanted out.

I wanted Icarus.

*I love Icarus.*

The King groaned in ecstasy. My eyes watered as he thrust again, not just from the intrusion but the violation. I knew the King had other priorities, that he was above humans in a way I couldn't fully understand, but this was a matter of caring *at all* for other living beings. He didn't have to take my suggestions for how we could make love, but this wasn't love at all. He didn't care whether I liked him fucking my mouth. Whether I could breathe.

I had no idea he could be so cruel. Dreams shattered. So many of them. People who cheered me on, and my own hope that I could make the King happier.

Another golden head lowered to take my place. When the King let go of me, I fell sideways onto the sky blue cushions, crying.

"I don't... feel well, my king. Please let me return later so I can please you better. I don't want to vomit on your..."

I really did feel like I would be sick. My gasp and gag must have convinced him, because he all but kicked me off the platform. He didn't say I'd be coming back.

My body felt heavy and foreign. I hated the gold and wished I had something to cover up. The sounds behind me turned my stomach. Were there others who felt like me still stuck with that monster?

Tears ran down my face as I traveled out of the room, downstairs again with the guard's help. I kept swallowing down my gag reflex.

Icarus wasn't there, so I walked alone back to the room as quickly as I could, arms crossed over my middle. He'd be waiting. He'd tell me what to do now. Maybe we could run away.

Because he'd never, *never* act like the King. He loved me.

And I loved him.

I'd been so wrong to put him second when he always put me first.

I was sobbing when the door came in sight. Sniffing, I blinked. The door was ajar.

"Hello?" Carefully, I pushed it open, in case anyone stood on the opposite side. "Hello?"

No one answered.

I tried to compose myself. My eyes had to look horribly swollen and the gold had probably rubbed off my lips. I scrubbed my entire face with the back of my hand and took three deep breaths before stepping through the curtains.

The place had been ransacked. Furniture lay all over the

floor. Feathers from pillows stirred lightly from my entering the room.

Panic seized me so hard I nearly collapsed. My limbs stiffened and sight narrowed to pinpricks that kept sliding out of focus. Where was Icarus? Was he killed? He couldn't be dead, couldn't be dead, couldn't be...

A rustling noise sounded from behind me.

I arranged my body to turn but everything was difficult. I couldn't speak.

A male guard stood there. "We just arrested your assistant. He was found with traitorous items in his possession."

I didn't understand. The words pinged off me. What traitorous items?

It didn't matter. He'd be killed all the same.

I made an inhuman noise of despair and rage.

The guard slammed my invention onto the tabletop in front of me. He'd done that enough times now that pieces had gotten loose. The clamp wouldn't line up with itself anymore if I tried to close it.

I squared my jaw at him, craving the ability to tear this place down around me. If my wrists weren't tied to the chair, I might have tried. The interrogation room was small enough—a closet by palace standards. Wooden instead of marble. Father sacrificed food so I could perfect that invention, and these people treated it like trash. Just like they treated Jacin.

"You know what this is," the man snarled in my face.

"A clamp." I wished I'd come up with a better name for it.

"A weapon." His mustache had one gray hair in it. "Weapons are not allowed in the palace."

My gaze dropped to the sword at his hip.

"Why did you bring it in?" he snapped, fiddling with some of the loose metal bits on the clamp. "Which group sent you?"

"No group—"

Pain stung my eye as he slapped me.

"No group sent me," I repeated in a growl. "I signed up for a job. That's all. And *that*"—I indicated my invention—"was something I planned to show people once I got here."

"But you didn't."

"Because I didn't see many people. It's for defense. And metalwork." I closed my lips before I told them it could break swords. These bastards didn't deserve to know. Besides, if they tested it, the pressure points weren't right anymore. It wouldn't work.

"You thought the King's consort could use it?" the guard sneered.

"I didn't know I'd be his assistant," I bit back. "The notice only said there was a position at the palace."

"Who sent you to apply?"

"No one! You really think I could take on the palace with that?" I nodded at the clamp. If only I could.

The guard followed my eyeline dubiously. "The last group only wanted to start chaos, killed a few servants, painted obscenities on the wall."

My throat closed. *Poor servants.*

"Those kinds of plans get you killed." He blinked slowly, a clear indication that the last people who infiltrated the palace, whoever they were, met that fate. Unsurprising, when merely touching Jacin could result in instant death.

"I don't want to cause chaos. I want to get back to my job." I twisted my wrists in their bonds. "You can keep that."

The strongest thread connecting me to the Labyrinth, apart from Father himself, snapped with the words. A lifetime of inventing, culminating in this.

It had to be okay. Sometimes a lifetime worth of plans didn't mean those plans were always going to be the best. I didn't plan on Jacin.

The eye where the guard had hit me began to swell.

He regarded me for a few more moments before tucking the metal clamp under his arm. "If we so much as sniff disloyalty..."

*Why might anyone feel disloyal to this fair, perfect kingdom?*

I nodded.

"Go back, now," he said, as if he were dismissing a child.

I couldn't move until he untied me, but the message was clear. I wasn't in trouble anymore for some godsdamned imagined threat.

As soon as my bonds loosened, I snatched my hands out of the ties and stalked quickly from the room.

This day couldn't have been any fucking worse.

Hopefully Jacin was okay. Maybe I was wrong about how his first time with the King would go.

Either way, I needed to see him. That was a big moment for anybody, and he'd been looking forward to it for so long. He might want to talk. And I just wanted to look at him and know he was all right.

Our door still swung slightly open. Sighing, I shoved it with a finger and went in.

A loud gasp made me tense. Jacin, eyes filled with tears, ran forward and flung himself into my arms.

# 21

# JACIN

Icarus felt solid and sturdy and alive. His arms closed around me the instant we collided, holding me firmly against his body. A sob escaped my mouth and I let it puff against the crook of his neck.

"I'm here," he said, barring my back and running fingers through the hair at the nape of my neck with his other hand. He shut the door behind him with his foot.

My hands splayed, wanting to feel more of him. I didn't want anything else. Only this. Icarus in my arms. I held on tight as if he'd drift away.

The tension in my body melted as he held me. All the agony of the King's chamber and returning to Icarus's certain death eased slowly. Bit by bit. Replaced with the firm chest against mine, his scratchy beard against my cheek.

We could never let go. If I released him, we'd never touch again, and now that I'd crashed through that barrier, I knew I couldn't live without this.

Plus, Icarus would die. Maybe I would too.

As if he sensed my terrified thoughts, Icarus soothed, "Shh. Shh. This is worth it to me."

I coughed another sob.

He backed up, still holding me to him with one arm, so he could look at me. He was rugged and handsome this close. Even with the purpling eye, this was my favorite view of him, because it meant I got to share his air and we got to be real people to each other. Not just bodies from a distance. He smelled grimy, but I loved it.

His gaze darkened when he saw my face. He didn't ask what had happened or say he was right. He simply cupped my cheek—which felt so extraordinary, gestures like that couldn't possibly be normal—and rubbed under my eye with his rough thumb. He held my gaze the entire time.

*I love you.* The words sat on my tongue. I felt so much as I stared back at him, maybe he could tell.

He leaned forward.

My pulse jumped as if we hadn't already broken the most important rule. Getting closer now wouldn't break it more.

I met him halfway, leaning my forehead on his. His warm breath mixed with mine. Then his thumb soothed gently against my spine, and I chose.

I chose Icarus.

I chose death before the King.

I chose to kiss the one I loved.

Our lips met quickly—Icarus inhaled sharply through his nose. His hands on my back, holding me steady, and his lips, worshipful and searching, made me a glutton for more. As much as he would give me.

I moaned against his mouth. Icarus answered, squeezing

me tighter and kissing me deep and frenzied. Only he wore clothes, so it was easy to feel his hard on against my hip. Remembering what he'd said behind the curtain, I rolled my body against him.

"Oh fuck," he slurred against me.

We walked clumsily together over the wreckage of the room toward the big bed, like an animal with no idea how to use four feet.

I pressed into him with my lips, my body, anything I could use to touch him, to get closer. My fingers hooked in the back of his waistband. More clumsy tripping as we stripped off his pants without letting go of each other. My hand slid up the front of his shirt too. I felt the trail of dark hair.

Nothing existed beyond Icarus. I wanted him like I wanted air.

The first touch of his thigh against mine, his chest against mine, and I was harder than I'd gotten when we'd masturbated on opposite sides of that sheet.

I pushed him onto the bed. He grinned, sloppy and wicked. "How do you want me?" he breathed.

*Every way I can have you.*

And he was right. His muscles bulged in all the right places, like a laborer or an athlete. Each one couldn't be drawn, but they were perfect anyway. He didn't need to be leaner or more cut to attract me more. I wanted to lie on his muscles and lick them and have that thick arm hold me tight around the waist again.

"Turn over."

He did. I sprinted to the basket beside the bed and picked

out pleasure oils. Filling my palms to the brim, I slapped them down on Icarus's back.

He laughed. "I think those are for... exactly what you're doing."

Maybe I was using this wrong, but I couldn't care less. I wanted to touch every bit of his body until it was oily-slick. When I was less turned on, I'd go slower. For now, my hands raced up over his shoulders, down his generous ass, and firm thighs.

"Make sure some gets where you want to be," he rumbled, smiling.

Breathing hard, I slathered myself with oil as quickly as I could and tipped out the last of the bottle on Icarus's little hole.

He gasped again. I lived for that sound.

"Good?" I asked.

He gave a drunken nod.

I spread his cheeks with my hands in a buzzing haze of lust. Then, with a grunt, I pushed my way inside.

Icarus's groan of pleasure made me so hot I felt feverish.

"Yes?" I panted. He was so tight I wasn't sure I'd fit.

"Keep going."

I rolled my hips, making headway. The motion propelled itself until I was thrusting desperately into him, savagely, quick and hard. I ground against his ass, finally burying myself completely.

Icarus arched.

Grinding and straining against him, I tried to go deeper, to satisfy the throbbing ache for more. Guttural noises burst from me with every thrust.

"Oh fuck!" Icarus cried again. He exhaled on a laugh. "Ah, fuck, that's right!"

I was mad for him.

"I want to see your face," I said.

"What?"

"I want to see your face."

I pulled out of him so he could flip over. There were the eyes I loved. Gods, I even loved the little trail of hair.

He reached out so he could hook my neck and pull me down for a kiss. "Take control. Take all of me," he murmured humid into my mouth.

"I want to see you. And I want to touch you."

"Leg okay?"

Now it was my turn for confusion. "What?" Then I realized. I hadn't given my injured leg a thought. I hadn't even remembered the gold paint, but now I noticed it smeared on Icarus's backside. "No. It's fine. Let me in again."

He tucked up his legs to give me better access. That way I could lean on them if I wanted to, or stand, or pump his cock, or all three. I was mostly focused on lining myself up in the right spot to drive into him, but I caught him watching me. Awe and pride lit his features. And animal lust.

I wanted him crazy, like me. Every tiny point of contact lit up my skin like lightning.

My cock sliding into his perfect ass.

His shins against my chest.

The brush of his fingertips against the back of my hands as I braced myself, as if he was checking to make sure we could still touch.

I caught his shaft and made it match my ruthless speed. In

and out. Up and down. I needed to take him with me as I grew wilder. Need drove everything I did. My hand wasn't right without his cock in it, shorter and thicker than mine. I had to know it, know the length and places that made him gasp and curse and grip the blankets. I needed to follow that trail of hair down his chest to his groin, know the texture. I needed to tease him. To fuck him until the world didn't exist.

I barked out my anger and desire as I pounded harder.

"Yes!" Icarus's voice was nothing but a hoarse whisper now.

My balls contracted. I couldn't hold off what was coming.

It was like he knew. He drew our faces together into a kiss made of too much teeth and sweat as we strained and released.

# 22

## ICARUS

I was so proud of Jacin.

And not just because he had a god's stamina. While I still flopped on the bed, drenched in sweat and oil after our earthshaking sex, Jacin perked up again after one post-orgasm kiss. He needed two minutes. I needed more, but I was determined to give him every speck of pleasure I could.

He deserved it. He'd taken back his life.

When I offered to suck him off despite being woozy and satisfied myself, he frowned at me. "You don't have to do that."

"Trust me, I want to. I've wanted to since I first met you."

He blushed and let me lie between his legs. I always thought I was good at blow jobs, although I hadn't given one in approximately a thousand years. It turned out I was right. Jacin had an obsession with my tongue. The way he shook and begged for more would haunt my wettest dreams.

When I was done, he pulled me up beside him and kissed me. We held each other. Any time the silence stretched enough to let in the question, we'd go in for another fuck.

Anything he wanted to try. Mostly, it was emotional, clinging, desperate thrusts with an orgasm so intense we shouted.

Eventually, we had to drink water. And we were filthy with cum, gold, and oil. Spit was in there too. Maybe some scratches. So we moved debris out of the way and filled the tub.

Jacin had a new resolve to him now. I leaned back against his chest in the bath, letting all the scented oils steep around us. He played with my chest hair under the water. I never thought I'd be glad for a break from having his body tangled with mine.

"I love you," he said, and kissed my neck.

The sweet press of his lips to my pulse made a rock lodge in my throat. "I love you more, I bet. I'm so proud of you." The fingers stroking my chest changed their rhythm. I felt his smile dimple against my nape.

Then the question got in.

*What now?*

"We should escape," I said.

"How?"

Relief had no room after coming so hard with Jacin, but I was glad he didn't push back against my suggestion.

"I don't know, but we should do it now." I craned back to look at him. "Have you ever left the room for something other than your... meetings?" I refused to mention *that name* in this sacred space.

"No."

If Jacin was only paraded outside the room as a nude golden statue, hardly anyone would notice who he was if he wore some of my clothes, would they? The outfits would be too short on him, but I could probably find something...

"I want to do something to hurt the King," he said quietly.

I nodded. Something bad had happened in that room after I left. I couldn't focus on it or else I'd get distracted with thoughts of how to kill an unkillable god. If and when Jacin wanted to talk to me about it, I'd listen. "I do too."

An idea started clicking into place like pieces of a machine.

I rubbed the top of his leg. "Let's go. They'll deliver food soon, if they're still doing that for us." I looked out over the ruined room. "Let's not make it easier for them to order an execution. And I think I might have an idea."

## 23

# ICARUS

I peered out into the hallway. No one.

"The door's that way," I told Jacin, pointing to the right. "When you get to the end, just go through."

He widened the collar of the oversized brown coat I'd chosen from my clothes. The fabric was rough, and Jacin kept adjusting it. It was harder to find Jacin shoes, since he normally didn't wear any. His feet were bigger than mine, so the best I could do was lend him my socks and tie some straps of leather over the top to fool the eye.

He pulled the door shut with us inside his room.

"Jacin," I pleaded.

He kissed me firmly on the mouth. His hands bracketed my face. "Don't let anything happen to you."

"I won't." It wasn't a promise I could keep, but he needed to hear it. "Just walk confidently once you get outside. No one will stop you. There are hundreds of people with business at the palace. Nobody will have any idea you don't belong."

My attempts to make him less attractive only made him

look messy and beautiful. Good thing the coat had a hood. The fewer eyes on him, the better.

There was little I could do about my own black eye. I had no choice but to play myself. If I stayed here, I'd be murdered. This way, at least I had a chance.

"You'll find me?" he asked again.

"Yes. Just keep walking straight as you can until you're outside the palace grounds. Keep going."

*With or without me.*

He kissed me again, his hand sliding down to intertwine with mine.

"We have to go," I said, throat scratchy.

He bit his lower lip and released my hand. With a deep breath and a heart-stopping half-smile, he nodded.

Gods, I wanted to stay. I wanted this to work out for us. But even if it didn't, I regretted nothing.

"You first," I whispered, opening the door for him.

As he walked away, his back looked nondescript covered in my coat. This could work.

Now it was my turn. I stepped out into the abandoned white hallway. Lovely music mocked me as it floated through the air.

*For Jacin.*

I turned left, toward the Sun King's chamber.

THE GUARD WASN'T EXPECTING ME.

Exactly as I hoped.

No one else stood in this alcove, unlike in the musician's hall. Maybe this pillar was used only for the King's consorts. Doubtful that King Lox had official meetings in a room that smelled like sex.

My ears strained to hear footsteps approaching. Did the tall female guard have the same power as the Guardian had? Would she be able to tell I'd been with Jacin?

It was always a risk. And she had that godsdamned club to use if I was wrong.

*Clack, clack.* Boots on marble floor.

Hopefully she wouldn't notice the new sheen.

I bowed my head humbly as she appeared. Her leather and metal armor looked thicker than I remembered, though it was probably the same.

"What are you doing here?" she snapped.

"My most excellent ray, the Sun God's favorite, left something behind in the chamber that he needs to retrieve. He's terribly sorry."

"That's not—!"

I looked up in time to see her eyes fling wide, foot slipping on the veneer of "fine oil for the King's play" I'd spread across the floor.

From my angle, I could see the dry spot I'd left for myself, and I threw myself forward. She fell hard, sliding half her body length toward the pillar.

Heart thrashing, I bent to tug out the gnarled staff and bludgeon from her belt.

She reached up and squeezed my throat so hard, its insides rasped together.

Choking, I worked the bludgeon from its holster. Demigods could die, couldn't they? Maybe she was one of those. At least I'd try to take her out with me.

With all my strength, I swung the club upward against her arm. It crunched and she compulsively let go. I flung the bludgeon down again, directly at her face. She didn't have time to block me.

I looked away when it made contact, leaving it lodged there and scrabbling for the gnarled staff instead. She might revive. A human couldn't survive that, but deathless beings could.

I hyperventilated, my fingers growing numb. Sickness climbed to the back of my throat.

One more stop.

I clutched the short staff in my fists, willing the darkness to crush me upward to the King's chamber.

But nothing happened.

*Fuck.*

My mind was a blank. The staff didn't work? Did it need the guard alive and awake to make the trip?

*Oh gods, no.*

Only after I started running on legs that didn't feel like mine did I realize that deathless beings in the music-filled hall might notice I had blood on my hands. Furiously, I wiped them off on my clothes. *Should I keep the staff? Would they need it to transport me up?*

My mind whirled in erratic circles.

"You!" I cried when I encountered the first person. She was taller than Jacin, robed, with thick strands of fire-orange hair and big freckles across her nose. Deathless.

She met my eyes and her brow furrowed. "Is something wrong? What's wrong?"

"I need to get to the King's chamber. The one above the pillar. An emergency." I ran out of breath.

Every second hurtled me closer to the moment someone found out the truth and cut off my head. I felt like I'd jumped off a mountain and was trying to maneuver as the air screamed around me.

"That's only for his private meetings," she said.

"I'm the assistant to his excellent ray, the King's favorite, Jacin. He's... not well, but he left something important in the chamber. I went to fetch it and found..." I pressed a hand to my chest and discovered I still held the gnarled staff.

The deathless woman didn't appear surprised by that fact.

"If the King wishes it..." she said uncertainly.

"I think there might be a new attack," I whispered. The shock of the violence was starting to harden into a calm I could work with. "Come and see."

She peered furtively around. As I suspected, she didn't call out for new guards. The palace thrived on secrecy and the impression that everything was good always.

"Follow me." I hurried back down the hall toward the pillar.

She screamed, covering her mouth.

"That's what I saw," I said, refusing to look at the guard I'd mangled. "I need to get to the King's chamber to make sure he's safe."

She reached out a hand and I took it.

Darkness.

Light.

I opened my eyes. The deathless woman, almost before I could turn to thank her, said, "Good luck," and left.

I had only moments. My nerves tingled, but I stumbled forward onto the cushioned platform. If I jumped, I could reach the cluster of globe lights illuminating it. I plucked them each down like fruit from a tree. Magic lit them, but magic using actual balls of fire. I smiled.

And smashed the globe lights one by one, putting all my strength behind each throw. My anger at what the King had done to Jacin and what he was doing to these other young men.

"Fuck you, and fuck this!" I hissed, slamming the last one against the spot where the King had forced a kiss on Jacin.

The balls of flame didn't go out when the glass broke. They clung to the surfaces where I'd thrown them. Madly, I ripped apart the stained, sky-blue pillows and fed the flames with their insides. Fire began to crackle and burn all over the room.

Along the far wall, water trickled down carvings of King Lox. I hurtled toward the feature, reaching up to feel where the waterfall began. There. A slit in the rock. I used the empty pillow fabric to jam into the crack and stop the water. A little leaked through, but not enough to stop the blaze, which licked higher and higher.

I tossed the gnarled staff on the biggest flame. The room was hot, dark with smoke. I coughed and kept going. No one would use this place again.

The smell of smoke filled my nostrils and went to my head. Most of the fires reached up to my waist or above. My eyes burned.

I had to get out.

Doors lined the circumference. If those didn't lead down...

I yanked on the first handle. Locked. Kicking the door hard didn't budge it either. I coughed a heaving, lung-deep cough.

I had known this was a possibility. I never told Jacin, but I knew I could die getting justice for him. There was no better way to go.

Holding my breath and struggling to see through the thick haze, I tried the second door. No. The third. The handle burned my palm.

But it turned.

Giddy with relief, I plunged inside, shutting the door behind me. The dark space felt sultry-hot, but far less smoky. I held my arms out to my sides to feel the space. A wall there, another on the other side. I took a step forward.

Exploring as quickly as I could, I shuffled forward through the dark. Then my foot hit air and I tripped, banging my knee on the hard edge of a step and roughly falling down a few more.

Stairs. I blinked away sooty tears and laughed. Once I got the rhythm of the spiral staircase, I flew down, not even annoyed when I smacked into a hard barrier at the bottom. I felt blindly for—there!—a handle. I emerged into a hall identical to the one I lived on with Jacin. That meant...

I broke into a run. Someone opened a door set into the wall to see what the commotion was about. I sprinted past them, hurling myself toward the end of the hallway.

When I took my first step into the sunlight, I nearly vomited with relief. The palace gardens and paths zigzagged like a paradise in all directions. I didn't see Jacin.

I squinted as I slowed my pace to a ferociously fast walk. Signs pointed me back to where I'd first entered the palace. That was where I'd find him.

My legs ate up the distance past gardeners, the goldsmith shop, trees with golden fruit... My chest ached with smoke, but I moved as quickly as I could without arousing suspicion.

No one stopped me. A few people hurried past in the direction of the palace. I smelled fire, but that could have been the odor clinging to my clothes. I didn't slow.

Finally, I made it past the palace grounds and turned toward where I knew Jacin should be. My skin stung from the heat of the royal chamber, but I didn't care. I didn't care about anything but him.

The most logical exit radiating from our part of the palace would be right there. It was a gold-plated garden gate constructed between two large hedges. I finally slowed my pace a little.

People went about their business around me, but none were shaped like him.

I meandered along the path leading from the gate, searching every face and figure. I'd gotten out, and I probably looked like a criminal. He had to have made it if I'd gotten this far.

Around a huge trunk to the side of the path, a young man stood with simple wonder on his face. As if he couldn't help but pause, his head tipped up to admire the sunlight filtering through the leaves.

"Jacin."

He grinned that huge, open smile that first made me fall in

love. "Icarus," he whispered back, scooping me in for a tight hug. "You made it."

"Let's keep walking," I said around my tight throat. We found each other's hands.

"The sun," he said after we'd taken a few steps. "It's more beautiful than I remember." He gave my fingers a squeeze as he looked up.

I had no eyes for the sunlight, only Jacin. "Yes," I said. "It is."

# 24

# EPILOGUE: ICARUS

I double-checked the measurements and set the clamp against the metal piece. It gave with a splintering crack when I squeezed the handle. Keeping a shoulder in place was more difficult than setting a calf, like I'd done with Jacin. The knee joint bent only one way.

I lifted the metal and set it against my own shoulder, bulkier now that I'd been back in the Labyrinth for a while. Jacin and I had so many customers, they kept us busy most days. I created the splints, slings, and sometimes false limbs, and Jacin massaged torn muscles and smoothed numbing agent or warming oils over people's skin when they were in pain. Together we handled many kinds of injuries. Our shop was popular enough that I owned my own smithy now, right behind the shop and home where I lived with Jacin. Father lived close enough to walk.

The morning sun slanted hard rays through the window. Combined with the heat of the forge, the smithy sweltered.

Better to get jobs like this finished early before the hottest part of the day.

I made a few more cuts to the metal with my re-built clamp, improved to work even on steel that wasn't the same shape as a sword. Leather clasps and rivets completed the project. I set it on a wooden stand and toweled off my chest before slinging on a shirt.

It felt cooler outside. A few steps through the trees got me to our back door. I entered quietly.

"Good morning!" came Jacin's bright voice. In the next room, he sat propped up in bed, reading a book with a cup of tea, a muffin, and a candle on the table next to him. "You're up early."

"So are you."

He set the book down and rose to join me. As usual, when we were at home, he wore only loose drawstring pants. "You know why?" he asked with an impish grin.

I chuckled, the memory coming back. "It's our day."

"Four years ago." He sidled closer and gave me a quick kiss.

We'd escaped the palace four years ago to the day. Whether they thought I'd died in the fire, I never knew. It didn't surprise me that no one came looking for Jacin. He was never the King's favorite, despite his pandering title. News that the King's consort had run off with a poor human could never reach his subjects. It was too great a stain on his golden image.

Jacin had filled in a little during those four years. Even simply reading in bed, he stole my breath every time.

"I wanted to do something for you," he said.

"Mm hm," I teased, pushing him backward.

"It's going to be very nice." His back hit the wall and he laughed. "I thought wax, a massage...?"

"Mm hm." I lined up my body with his and kissed him deeply. His arms wrapped around my sweaty back. I felt him smile against my mouth.

He was hard for me already. I rolled my hips against his. He gasped. The stiff line of his cock through his pants rubbed against mine with delicious friction. I did it again. I'd never get used to how responsive he was.

"We could... ah, ah!... do the wax tonight."

I hummed into his mouth. "Perfect."

I bucked my hips faster, grinding relentlessly against his hard on. He held onto me with shaking arms.

Before I could explode on him, I slowed. My mouth felt gummy and face hot. He looked back at me, drunk with sensation.

"Let me do something first," I said, thumbing his bottom lip.

He nodded.

I knelt in front of him and slowly peeled down his pants. His cock flew out hard as a steel rod. I pulled down until he could step his bare feet out. With all the tenderness I felt, I curved my hand around the back of his calf and pressed my lips to his scars. Taking my time, I visited each one. They were different shapes and depths, and my lips paid homage to them all. Jacin stayed quiet enough that the only sounds were the morning birds and my kisses.

Easing my hand up the back of his leg, I kissed higher, licking, nipping now, but keeping my devotion soft. One kiss to the inside of his thigh, and then I finally moved on to his hard length, ready for me. I sucked the tip gently. Jacin braced himself flat-palmed against the wall.

Slowly, I ramped up the sensation, running my tongue along his shaft and pulling his balls into my mouth. Jacin started to shudder and whimper. Nothing in the world compared to making him fall apart like this. I slid him all the way into my mouth and down my throat.

Jacin convulsed. "Fuck!" he yelled loud enough for neighbors to hear.

I didn't stop. I'd draw every bit of pleasure from him until he was writhing and panting and couldn't stand. Soon, he was thrusting his hips as if he couldn't stop himself.

"I want to come in your mouth," he gasped.

In answer, I pushed him down my throat again.

"Fuuuuck!" He quivered so violently, I thought he'd break right there.

I braced myself by holding onto his thighs, just under his perfect ass, and met his thrusts with my own.

He sobbed and moaned with need. "Ah, yes!" he cried. "Fuck. Fuck, I'm coming. I'm—"

A thick stream of cum shot into my mouth. I swallowed, and more followed in bursts. I licked him clean and stood, smirking.

His body heaved, sweat trickling down his temples.

"You sounded like me," I said. "Watch your words."

At the edge of collapse, he fell against me, meeting my lips with his. He explored my mouth for his taste.

Then he broke away, lucid enough to smile again. "I'm glad I sound like you." He sighed. "You're *very* good at that."

My cheeks crinkled. I was so fucking lucky. Being with Jacin still felt like a fantasy.

He put his pants on again and kissed me on the forehead. "No waiting until tonight. Our next customer doesn't come for an hour. Your turn."

And he grabbed the candle.

# THANK YOU!

Thank you for reading *Candle Wax and Sunlight*! Please consider leaving a review. Reviews help authors like me get found by more readers.

Now, read on for a sneak peek of another story that will leave you begging for more...

Or, read *Wings and Blindness*—an Eros and Psyche remix that asks what would happen if Psyche were sent to kill Eros to begin with...

This first book in the Deathless Love series welcomes you to the Eight Realms, where danger and desire lurk in every corner, and mythology isn't quite as you remember it.

Join the Foxy newsletter and read this book FREE!

*What if the goddess Freya fell in love... twice?*

The goddess of beauty and strength isn't supposed to be like this. At least, that's what Freya thinks when she returns to her queendom after a long absence. Recovering from a terrible injury and now fighting to get her land back from her ex, she faces her greatest challenge: reclaiming herself.

Helping her is Kasir, a free-spirited traveler visiting the castle to cast protective barriers. Their chemistry is instant and addictive. Both used to short-lived flings, they burn through nights together, confident that he won't be tied down and she won't be trapped in another doomed relationship. After all, he plans to leave as soon as he finishes the job.

Flightiness is foreign to Weyland, who has worked on Freya's castle through generations. Freya has all his devotion, but guilt eats him up that he couldn't do more to protect her land from her vicious ex. His awkwardness stopped him until it was too late. He's convinced Kasir doesn't deserve her, but the more they're stuck together, the more he starts feeling a troublesome attraction toward the dashing warder.

Can Freya find beauty and strength in not only herself, but two lovers?

I hadn't been on one of these runs in fifty years. Cool air rushed past my exposed arms and chest. I hadn't bothered binding my long hair back. This run was supposed to make me feel more like myself. Before everything. And feeling my hair catch in the breeze, tickling my shoulder, felt more like me. I liked the sensuality of mare skin against soft hair.

Ashes and oaks passed like pillars. Fresh. Not like Urd in the south where I went to help a chaotic situation and got stuck healing for decades. Okay, it was partially to help. I'd have brought my Valkyrie guards if that were really the point.

I needed a break, a new place, space to breathe without Ivar. I picked up my pace, pushing my tired legs faster. This route through the castle grounds used to be refreshing. Now it pushed my hard enough that sweat rolled down my back under the deerskin top and my legs burned.

Just over that rise. I could get a good view of the queendom I'd left leaderless. I hadn't done it on purpose. No one could have predicted the War Twins from the Eight Realms fighting over Urd and leaving most of the gods lying in pieces.

I was supposed to be the goddess of beauty and strength but the memory made me slow, my stomach roiling like snakes with queasy dread. Scars on my belly marred what had been so perfect that men and women begged to spend nights with me. Something else I missed. Strong and beautiful, I reveled in using my body for pleasure. Sub, dom, one, two, three—I liked it all when I found good partners.

Ivar was different. Dominant, through and through. I enjoyed it for a awhile, the gags and restraints, but then it wasn't just in the bedroom anymore. He spoke in commands. I could speak in commands too. He lived in *my* kingdom. Ivar had no right to push himself into positions of authority, but I'd found out after the fact. It was constant. The sex stopped, but the manipulation didn't. I was sick of it. Sick of him. Tired of dealing with him. I kicked him out of the kingdom and heard Urd was in trouble—a great excuse to get away for a while. A different kind of trip for me. This one wasn't for fun and adventurous sex. Instead, it was the opposite—a total break, hopefully with nothing to remind me of the headache that was Ivar.

The rise appeared through the trees. My favorite spot. I needed that view today. At least I made it the entire way. Bryn had suggested that I appreciate small victories: my scars hadn't opened for a few months, I was strong enough to run at all, I was back now, even if everything that gone to hell while I was gone and I couldn't sleep without waking up ten times with anxieties or flashbacks or anger so fierce I felt it burn.

A white square, like some kind of sign, showed on the cliff overlooking the kingdom. I frowned and slowed. This was my land. If Ivar had set up signs on my property, I'd throw them in his face.

Two squares, side by side. My fingers closed int fists.

A man sat in front of the parchments. It wasn't Ivar. This person was leaner and his hair was shorter.

One square showed a half-completed recreation of the landscape—deep greens rolling into mountains and rocky valleys as far as the eye could see. The other held abstract forms in blackish-blue and deep reds, great swaths of paint that had no recognizable subject, but evoked a feeling anyway.

The man turned. Young or deathless.

"What are you doing here?" I doubted he was spying for Ivar. The subtlety of sending a painter was beyond him.

The man stood and inclined his head before gesturing to his work. "Painting, as you can see. I like to paint things twice. And you are, my lady?"

Confident. Confident without sounding cocky or condescending. "Queen Freya," I answered, trying out the name for the first time in too long.

Dimples formed in the man's cheeks. "I thought so." He smiled and bowed. "The red hair gave you away. You're as beautiful as they say."

I didn't feel as beautiful. I felt ripped and stretched, like an old toy that needed mending. The man's compliment sounded rote, but the way his gaze lingered on me suggested he believed the words.

He was about my height, lean, with short dark hair and sun-kissed skin. His face molded into easy creases that made his entire aspect welcoming and sensual at once. His eyes sparkled with stories. Paint dotted his knuckles. He didn't wear the typical browns and brass and leather of Varafjall but loose-fitting pants that might be worn in the east and a form-fitting blue shirt—long-sleeved for sitting on this cool day. The fabric hugged the contours of his arms and chest in a way that made me want to run my hands over them.

"I don't typically allow strangers to paint on castle grounds unless they're invited," I said.

"You invited me, my queen. I'm the warder."

I'd forgotten about that. Weyland, my metalsmith, had told me the wards had weakened, so I called for a warder from Hyperion to come to Castle Mist once he was finished in Urd.

"Kasir" I guessed.

"Here to help." He flashed another easy smile.

"Why didn't you come straight to the castle?"

Again, he indicated his artwork. "Figured I could create a souvenir of the trip before I have to leave. If you'd like, I can pack this up. The paint's still wet, so..."

"No," I said, coming closer. Kasir didn't retreat when I stepped forward. It had been ages since I flirted with anyone. Ivar had stolen that essential part of me. Kasir was leaving. No harm in a little fun. It'd be good for me. I missed my body. I missed my power. I missed *me*.

Trailing my fingers along his toned upper arm, I regarded the paintings. "Why do you make two of them?"

"One isn't enough." His eyes twinkled as he side-eyed me. "One is for the landscape itself and the second is for the way it makes me feel."

I looked at the sweeps of dark blue and red. I'd always thought of dark red as my color—the color of beauty, strength, and feminine sensuality. "You feel... how?"

"Excited to begin. Calmed by the beauty here, but ready for adventure," he answered, a question in his eye.

Warmth trickled down my neck and chest. Such invitation in those eyes. "Ready?" I repeated, prompting him to go on.

"For whatever comes in this job. The last one was stressful, but I like a few bumps. The landscape here is perfect enough that I could stare at it for hours." But he wasn't staring at the landscape.

His words would have sounded cheesy if I hadn't felt the heat coming off them. Bold of him to flirt so openly. I liked it. Terrible that I needed the push, but that was exactly what I needed. "It's been a while since I had a few bumps," I purred.

"Yeah?" His grin was wicked. Here was somebody who liked a good romp as much as I did.

Gorgeous, willing partner? Leaving in a few days? He was perfect for my first foray back.

"Sit down," I ordered. "This painting"—I indicated the abstract one—"I want to feel like this. Can you show me?"

Kasir sat and beckoned me onto his lap. I obliged. He released a quiet breath into my hair that set my blood boiling. "This here," he said low into my ear, reaching past me to point at his work, "is how I feel right now. An ache to begin. Excitement. Is that what you want me to show you?" His hand closed around my waist to hold me in place on his lap. He didn't know about the deep scars there.

I rolled my hips. "Exactly."

When I tipped my head back, he brought his lips to my neck. "Perfect. My gods, you're beautiful." This time, the compliment gusted out with desire, not the automatic inflection from last time.

"Then show me how I make you feel."

Underneath me, he adjusted his hips, pressing his bulge against me.

"More," I demanded. My hands traveled up to his cheek, pushing his head so our lips connected. His breath was humid and insistent. It had been too long. I loved this.

He explored the front of my body, running his palms over

my stomach and breasts. My skin heated until the chill didn't matter. I hooked my thumbs in my waistband and pulled down. As soon as I was bare, with my pants halfway down my thighs, he frantically fiddled with his own clothes. Seconds later, he eased out his stiff cock, holding it so I could settle on top. Wet enough to compensate for the slight tightness, I lowered myself onto him. He gave miniature thrusts to get further in. The slide of his cock as he entered me erased everything else. All that remained was the hard, heavy length of him inside me, the shuddering breaths he took as he adjusted to me, the buck of his hips as he drove into me.

He held me in place as we rocked. I reached for more to satisfy that ache inside me, rubbing my ass back and forth against him. His panting turned into strangled laughter. It was a compliment. I was good at this. Even this makeshift position that didn't allow me to open my legs.

I rose up, holding myself just above his lap so he could smack harder, more desperately into me. A cry blew from my lips. He went faster.

Soon, I was all slippery heat and he was all masculine ache and we were rubbing, rubbing, rubbing, searching for that spot that would make us break. More sweat rolled down my back as I arched. His hands went everywhere, finally finding that place between my legs.

He groaned loudly, close. I echoed him. His fingers flicked my clit as he rolled his hips relentlessly into me.

My mouth opened, eyes shut, belly clenched and... I gave a high-pitched noise as I came and he ground out curses as his trembling arms tightened around me. I felt him shoot inside me.

Our bodies relaxed, a joined mass of sweat and satisfaction. I slid off him and managed to pull up my pants. He gazed appreciatively.

Gods, I'd chosen well. He clearly knew how to use that thing.

But the glow from our sex was already starting to wear off. My castle was crumbling, the wards were weak, and Ivar had taken possession of the kingdom I could see so clearly from this clifftop.

"This place is so much better than the last one," Kasir said with a sloppy smile. He tucked himself back into his pants and stood slowly.

I gave him a kiss. "We can walk back together once your paint dries. I want you to meet Weyland and get started on the wards."

He tossed his head. "Of course. You can tell me what kinds you need."

Warders were rare and valuable. He was brave to be out in an unknown wilderness alone, especially with Ivar's new reign still unstable. The humans who worshipped him might attack or spy on his behalf. Well, I'd make sure my castle and my lands had the best protection before I kicked his ass out and, hopefully, found my old strength again.

"How long will you be here?" I asked Kasir.

"It usually takes a week or two to solidify wards. Why?" He smirked.

We both knew why.

*BEAUTY AND IRON* IS COMING OUT SOON!

# READ MORE BY ZORA FOX

Fae and Shadow duology
*End of the Forest*
*Trapped by the Fae*

Deathless Love series
*Wings and Blindness*
*Flowers and the Far Realm*
*Storm and Sanctuary*
*Flame and Warpaint*
*Full Moons and Vampires*
*Temptation and Tridents*
*Candle Wax and Sunlight*
*Beauty and Iron* (coming soon!)

Find all of Zora Fox's spicy fantasy romance titles on Amazon.

www.ingramcontent.com/pod-product-compliance
Lightning Source LLC
Chambersburg PA
CBHW021727190726
48289CB00008B/2727